THE COMPANIONS

C. S. LUIS

CONTENTS

In the Empire, the Imperial forces are separated into three equal groups; the Imperial officers who serve the Empire, their Commanding officers who enforce the regulations and Admiral Patrick who presides over these divisions. These are their stories...

ARRIVAL

Resting near the railing, I was enjoying the crisp air blowing from the open viewport overlooking the beautiful forest greenery below. Like an open gallery, a section of windows lined the entire corridor. The cold air was allowed to flow freely through the interior, and I always liked the idea of passing my time here, just thinking.

The Station Victoria lay quiet this evening, except for a few commanding officers here and there conducting class. A group of cadets marched near me and a few other off-duty officers scaled the nearby rails to my right and left, examining the forest below. They looked restless, as if awaiting something. Their restless bodies edged closer to the rails and their enthusiastic eyes pierced the surrounding corridors in search and in longing. *What were they looking for?* I could only wonder.

It was close to the end of the year. The first signs of winter had been obvious for weeks, leaving an icy kiss on the Station's corridor. The chilly winds had started to blow—soon it would be time for the winds to stop whisking throughout the corridor. The cheerful comfort of the breeze would have to end, for it would soon be too cold to keep the windows open. I knew I would miss that, but the drapes would be drawn and I would have to adapt.

The corridor opened into a large interior space and, in the center, there were sitting areas and tables, a recreational area to pass the time, more than anything else. It was a perfect setting for reading a novel, catching up with assignments or just lying back and having a quiet conversation. I had used this place to hide away from the daily demands of military life. To find comfort in the peace that was difficult to acquire during the long stretch of time one did in Victoria. One could consider military life to be like hard time in prison.

Once again, other officers near the rails caught my attention, their smiles reflected the excitement exploding from their faces. It was obvious something was happening. My head lifted, and my eyes were drawn towards the entrance carefully watching the doors. I could almost sense the atmosphere change around me; the other officers sensed it too.

In that moment, the new recruits entered. Strong youthful fresh faces, men dressed in their cadets' navy-blue uniforms, marching into the Station under the commanding officer's strict watch. However, it hadn't been these men in military uniform that captivated others, but those that followed right behind.

A line of beauties appeared through the entrance a step behind the cadets in perfect form, led by the scholars and perfectionists of obedience. The Royal Companions had arrived.

Standing near the entrance; my face turned slightly sideways as I noticed them just a short distance from me. My eyes, caught and bound by their perfect forms, had abandoned the beauty of the landscape down below for the more appealing sight behind me. I only had to turn to see the dozens of muscular young men being led into the corridor from where I stood.

The Station was especially for them, a place for learning and lecturing, as it was for the new recruits in uniform who were taught in a variety of classes concerning the basics of the Empire by Imperial officers like me. In fact, I had taught in some of the classes but had been out for the following two weeks on Imperial leave.

Sure, it was known Companions were trained for the pleasure of the Royals—trained to keep them company and submit to their every wish, no matter what. However, the *real* test was among the military personnel. The real challenge that would prove they were fit to become Companions of Royalty. Though only high-ranking officers were ever granted such a pleasure, sometimes the lower-ranking ones had the opportunity, when a disobedient Companion had to be disciplined. And these men here today, I thought, watching the batch of beauties enter, knew that and longed for the chance of just such an occasion.

In a momentary dreamy state, I saw him with the others. He was a lovely thing, dressed in royal blue— the color of a Royal Companion, which suited his smooth, bleached skin. His hair was long and red, like a fiery cape spread over his broad shoulders. He had a boyish face with a crooked smile and large gray eyes.

The robes of a Companion hardly concealed them and were worn to actually reveal certain parts of their bodies. The Companions' strong and muscular arms, along with their pale chests, seemed to invite and delight a quick purchase. The purpose was obvious—indulgence and seduction.

The redhead walked with the others; two single lines divided the Companions from one another. They were separated steps away from each other to keep them from making contact. Their hands were clasped against the backs of their necks, their eyes lowered, and always instructed to answer only when spoken to and obeyed.

They stopped near the entrance behind the marching cadets. The scholars encircled their students, carefully walking alongside them; each one on the opposite side of the lines to provide discipline where it was needed. The scholars were harsh and the sound of the whip against such beautiful skin delighted and widened their smiles.

The sound of the whip echoed in the cold, chilled corridor; faces remained still, yet eyes slightly swerved to catch a glimpse from those on the rails, and a few of the cadets. The lash struck two champion beauties immediately on the buttocks, however, with incredible control they lowered their gaze without so much as a quiver or whimper. It amazed me, how well-disciplined they were.

The scholars had done their work and, proudly, one of them turned in my direction as if noting my approval. One might have asked: Who were the scholars? Lower-ranking Imperial officers, perhaps, with the pleasure every man desired? To toy with young men, to tolerate their beauty and resist falling in love with them.

In fact, they were merely dark priests of seduction—students of the craft —a special order set forth by the Emperor. Admiral Patrick could have been considered one, a teacher perhaps, in the field of seduction.

Nonetheless, I won't get into the topic of Admiral Patrick, that's a different story altogether. However, I will say this, Admiral Patrick was too strict in his duties to ever consider such a delightful compliment, even though he had learned from one of the very best.

The scholars led the Companions away. It was then that the redhead's eyes caught sight of my longing stare. Only in that moment did I regret ever dismissing the chance offered by the Empire to consider becoming a Companion during my reassignment period. I was one of the very few ever given such an opportunity for my hard work.

I felt myself go limp as his eyes found me by the rails. The sparkles in his gaze sent a shock of pleasure to every inch of my body before it fell and abandoned me.

"Why did I refuse?" I clung to the rails as the pleasure passed through me.

Now it was too late and the hope of ever seeing such a chance was beyond my grasp. The best I could hope for was a promotion, or through good behavior to win myself another such opportunity. Who was I kidding—when such an opening was offered, one was a fool not to take it, and that's what I was, a fool.

Beyond the Station antechamber, officers walking by stopped to examine the newly arrived batch of beauties with awe. Immediate disappointment spread over their faces as a glare from the scholars and superior commanding officers seemed to remind them that they would be denied this pleasure, unless special discipline were required from lower-ranking officers.

The Companions marched and disappeared from

view, but I couldn't stop thinking about him. The wonder in his eyes, the gentleness in his step. For a Companion who was a willing servant, there was a sense of rebelliousness in his eyes with a need to be tamed by the right person.

There was also that conceited little smile spread over his face that was inviting as well as controlling. It had a great power over me, a force that was, without a doubt, overwhelming. The smile that said, "*Conquer me! Will you take the challenge?*" I certainly would, I thought with humorous delight.

I couldn't think, nor could I move—the feelings had frozen me in place. Only when I almost lost my balance and gripped the railings a tighter did I spot Commander Peterson approaching.

"Gabriel!" His soft voice called over to me. I gazed back as he stepped over to my side next to the railings, and I turned to immediately salute but stopped myself.

"Lieutenant, when did you get in?" There was a great amount of excitement in his voice. His eyes flashed at me into a delightful smile. He ignored my attempts to salute, giving me no time to answer, and embraced me tightly. Then laid a single kiss on my cheek, though I felt his intentions were to kiss my lips. He resisted this. So, like him to be such a professional officer, even with me.

Sometimes he reminded me of Admiral Patrick. And those thoughts alone hounded my mind and made me uncomfortable when I was around the Admiral, because I couldn't stop thinking about Eric in the same manner, bent in front of me in a position that would make anyone blush.

What did it take to win his approval? I only knew one man that had, the prince.

"Why didn't you send word you were coming back sooner?" Commander Peterson asked, looking slightly hurt and yet delighted to see me.

"I didn't expect to," I smirked, as he now rested his own hands on the railings next to me.

Bored and frustrated with civilian life, I frequent the civilian bars on nearby planets in search of adventure. Finally giving up I dragged myself back to the one place that could both entertain me and occupy me.

Commander Peterson's green eyes stared at me hard. I could sense how much he had missed me. The curve of my lips invited his longings, and rising desires, the ones obvious on his handsome face. Though older by a few years, Peterson—or Eric, his first name —didn't show his true age. Always a strict officer whose control over others had won him my admiration, respect and my love.

I was only 20 years old when I first came to the Empire; it was during the first months of training that I grew to know him and later fell in love with him. Back then it was he who led me like a lost puppy, but over time, things seemed different, and now I saw the same weakness in his eyes that had been in mine at the beginning of our relationship.

I curved my lips slightly, revealing the dimples on my cheeks—a feature that Eric said was the envied and admiration of others.

"I just got back. I couldn't take it anymore. I was bored out of my mind. There's nothing out there to do. Unless you want to roam the wastelands and local bars of Toliana. Not my thing."

"Ha! Ha! Your funny." Eric grinned, foolishly mocking.

"Besides, there's more drama here in the Empire than out there or anywhere in the galaxy."

"Is that a fact? Well, I'm one to agree with you on that." he chuckled, back with a crooked smile, and when he laughed, he was a handsome devil.

His full lips tucked in, and his eyes sparkled and became tearful. Like he hadn't had a good laugh in a long time. In fact, he had once said that I was the only one who could ever make him laugh, and now I could understand why. Before, his natural actions or his mannerisms never concerned me as they now seemed to.

"That's why I left the Zec a long time ago," he added, referring to the fact that most of the drama in the Empire was on board the Zec, and partially because of Admiral Patrick. In that sense, he was not far from the truth, but I never joined in when he indirectly meant to insult the Admiral, whom I held in high esteem.

When I didn't laugh, he fell silent, and as I glanced toward the window, he edged closer.

"I have time to spare before I have to go back on duty. I'd like to spend it with you, if I can. I've missed you dearly, Gabriel. I honestly didn't expect to see you return so soon."

Eric smiled warmly, drawing his hand closer until it was resting upon mine.

He then gripped my hand. He would have kissed it if we had been alone, but again, his professional demeanor kept him in place. On Station Victoria he was as well-respected as he was hard-working, known in the Empire as a devoted officer esteemed by his peers and colleagues. Yet, when we were seen together, there was always envy in the eyes of others. I was regarded as the handsome one. I was sure my good looks were the cause of the cruel unspeakable whispers and rumors about me.

When I came forward with these claims to Eric, he insisted people were jealous of our relationship and to ignore them. But I couldn't—I simply couldn't. These things enraged me, so that over a period of time I couldn't concentrate on my work and became a nervous wreck. Eric, worried and concerned about my health, took it upon himself to silence the rumors. Once again, he became the cruel and harsh gentleman officer that had driven the arrow into my heart. He had salvaged the remainder of my dignity, for what it was worth, and showered me with apologies—as if this had somehow been *his* fault. I assumed, in a sense, he was partially to blame for not stopping the rumors before they had escalated.

"How can I? I just got back," I uttered, but was it that?

I could easily walk back with him to his private chambers and do as I pleased. I had no one to report to but him, and he could so easily make up an excuse for my absence if I needed it.

In the past, it was I who begged him for a moment of his love, it was I who wanted his company and I who didn't care about regulations and those irritating rules and concerns. Now things had changed, and it was he who had put aside his rulebook and concerns to be with me.

His gaze fell upon me, and it seemed the desires boiling inside him would no longer remain hidden. Just then I felt that if I didn't give in to his wishes, he would drop into my arms sobbing like a helpless child.

"You know you don't need to concern yourself with that."

Of course, I knew that, but what delighted me more? The very fact he asked me, or seeing how easily he would break his own rules simply to be with me?

"Yes, I know," I whispered, turning away from

him, longing for an excuse to wander from him and see what trouble I could find on my own now that I had returned.

I was bored. Bored with how easily I could manipulate him. Bored with the idea that I could get away with just about anything.

"Don't you miss being with me?" he immediately and boldly asked, so that it surprised me as well as impressed me.

I wondered whether he was slowly growing tired of my distance or simply realizing what a fool he had been to allow me such freedom over him.

"Of course, I do," I answered slowly—hesitating was a habit of mine when answering him.

"Then, what's wrong? Are you upset with me?" he asked again, sounding as tame as a pussycat.

The hopes faded from me as I continued to gaze out the huge viewports of Station Victoria at the arriving vessels and the shouts of officers all around us interrupting the flow of my own thoughts.

"No, of course not. It's nothing really. I guess all I really need is some excitement, that's all. I left here hoping to find something out there, but I was disappointed when I didn't. Now I feel like I'm back to where I started."

I tried to look up at him and, again, my innocent eyes had overpowered him, and he now wrapped his arms around me.

"Are you sure that's all that's bothering you and

that it has nothing to do with us? Let's face it, we didn't see eye to eye before you left. I didn't want you to leave angry with me, but I also didn't want to stop you from doing whatever you wanted to do. I want to protect you, but I know I can't always."

He pressed his lips inward and lowered his eyes.

Only then could I see his true age and wisdom as the words poured from his lips and from the features of his firm expression. He seemed fatherly and nurturing.

"No. No, it's not you. It's me. Sometimes I don't know *why* I do the things I do—nor why you put up with me."

I actually felt like a spoiled lover, nuzzling to his older lover, clinging to him for protection and understanding, as only he could give to one as wickedly handsome as me. One who could so easily convince, with loving embraces and innocent eyes, an older man whose only fear was to be left alone.

"I do," Eric smiled. "It's because you are dear to me and I love you."

He squeezed me close and held me tightly.

"So, it's excitement you seek?" he smirked. "Then why are we waiting around here? Let's go somewhere we can be alone together."

He gazed down at me and planted a kiss upon my forehead, pressing me closer. I could feel the strain beneath his uniform's slacks rest against my own leg.

The desire coursed through him as he held me, and the tremble of his body beneath my touch.

I stared back at his loving green eyes. *Not at all what I had in mind,* I thought, but perhaps the time would ease my own desires and the thoughts of the young redhead Companion that still lingered in my loins.

However, the more I thought of him, the more I wanted him, and the more Admiral Patrick continued to haunt my awakening dreams.

As soon as we entered his chambers, he launched onto me, burying his hungry lips on my. He didn't even wait until we were completely inside, or for that matter, undressed. Usually, it was he who prolonged our moments. He who left me desiring him as he slowly made his way to me. Throwing me upon the bed or pinning me against the wall to satisfied himself. But this time, it was a completely different story, and it was he who would satisfy me, simply because he wanted me by his side.

I wasted no time, already feeling myself hard. Unzipping my pants, I ripped the trousers from his body. He voluntarily turned for me as I pushed into him and began riding him with devilish pleasure, grabbing his already hardened prick and began to pump it within my grasp, moving in the same satisfying rhythm.

He spread himself across the wall, his arms extended, his buttocks exposed outward, firm as I held him to me.

"Yes!" he cried out, through gasps and moans.

It should have excited me, but instead, I longed for harsh words and punishment from him. Instead of weak, boyish whimpers, I longed for spankings, longed for his pinches and those slaps that delighted me during our outrageous lovemaking. The moments he demanded to see me, only to punish me in his quarters with others a door away from what took place, others who could have so easily walked in on us.

I loved those moments. However, now it was all gone, and he had been tamed, and now it was *he* who would fall to his knees before me.

I collapsed on him in ecstasy as he buckled beneath me, his face pressed against the wall and his eyes closed. He took a deep breath and reached back to put his hand over my buttocks.

"Tie me up, Gabriel. Bind my hands together and ride me once more, I want you beside me again. Don't leave; let's stay here this evening. We don't have to go back on duty."

I pushed gently off him as he turned immediately to gaze back at me, wrapping his arms around my waist. His hungry wet organ had hardened again, and I could feel it touching my bare buttocks.

"No." Removing his arms from around me. At

first, that's all that came from my mouth as I moved to gather my clothes from the floor.

"What?"

He moved towards me and took hold of my arm. I slowly turned to meet his confused expression, as his tall muscular form stood naked before me.

"I can't. Not now," I said bowing my head, as I turned away, silently hoping he would not ask me again, but I couldn't expect him not to.

"Why?"

I tried not to look at him, but it was hard. He turned me to him once more and, as my expression met his, I saw the pain I was causing him by not being truthful.

"I have to go to Station Delta. I leave after the auction tomorrow evening," I said, pulling up my trousers and fastening my belt.

The auction in reference was the purchase of the Companions. Everyone would be there to watch the great sale and to see the beauties displayed before the crowd of hungry Imperial eyes. It was the biggest thing held on Station Victoria, and those few commanding officers with the opportunity of buying a Companion came to do so. There were rumors that the Prince would come, but those were never true; what was believable were the rumors of Admiral Patrick making an appearance—or a maintenance check as he liked to refer to it—rather than coming for the celebration. Let's face it, he was more into this than he wanted people to believe, and that's what I liked about him. It only made me wonder what secrets lay untold in his personal world.

"What business do you have there?"

Again, I tried to avoid his eyes, but it was hard to keep my feelings from showing to someone who already knew certain gestures that gave me away when I tried to lie. I didn't answer right away, but then I wasn't even sure myself what exactly had me heading in the direction of Station Delta.

"What are you seeking, Gabriel?" he finally asked.

I didn't answer right away, perhaps frustrated that he simply had to know every bit of my business.

"I want to be someone, I want..." I fell silent and rushed to put on my uniform jacket to try to avoid further questions.

"What do you want? Do you even know what you want?"

"I want to be more than your little love toy! I want to be someone important!"

I held in the tears, pushed them back as hard as I could until I felt a lump in my throat aching to escape.

"You are important, Gabriel! You're important to me!"

"I want to be more than that! I want others to know it. I want recognition! I'm tired of living in your shadow!"

"Recognition from who? You're important to me, isn't that enough? My shadow?"

"NO! You don't understand!"

I rushed to the exit and he followed me to the access door and took hold of my arm again. I pulled away, slapping my officer's cap over the strands of my blond mane.

"Gabriel, stay and talk to me, don't push me away. Please."

I couldn't even look him in the eyes as I stood before him by the access door. He reached over to caress my cheek. I tried to avoid his touches as a sigh escaped my lips, and without a word, I turned from him and left him standing alone in his chambers.

THE AUCTION AT STATION VICTORIA

It was the day of the auction and everyone was there. I saw people I had never seen before, commanding officers I had only heard of, roaming the celebration grounds greeting one another. The ranks were, in a sense, forgotten here, though we were separated from the higher-ranking officers, who had their own private booth in the Station's auditorium, while the lower-ranking Imperial officers stood below them, watching the center stage and discussing the event in hand.

If I had played my cards right, I could have been sitting among the commanding officers in their private booth with Eric, but instead I had now settled to be alone among a group of shouting, unintelligent and disorganized lower-ranking officers.

I wasn't very popular with any of them. I knew

how they referred to me; some said I was spoiled. But then again, they would say that because they were jealous that Eric loved me. Jealous that he would give me the world. Though all I ever wanted was some respect.

I spotted Eric in the booth chatting with other superior officers, a commanding officer named Simpson, and another by the name of Armstrong. I had never spoken to either man but had been introduced to them once by Eric during Imperial gatherings or private parties that I had been able to attend as his guest.

I pushed the long bangs from my eyes. Officers beside me enviously frowned in my direction and whispered to one another. I tried to ignore what I could only imagine they were saying about me. Let's face it, they were simply jealous of my beauty and what gifts I had received because of it.

I looked up at the booth again. Perhaps now I regretted choosing to be down here among the unprofessional and unimportant low-lives of the Empire. This time, I caught Eric looking over at me from his seat up in the booth. The commanding officers beside him caught sight of me as well and their faces became firm and plain. Perhaps they were jealous too that Eric spent too much time with me, sometimes neglecting even a night out with buddies. Or was it that they were envious of him? Seeing what a prize he had won himself.

Most of the commanding officers were older gentlemen who couldn't get a date or a pretty face unless they were willing to spend plenty of money to have one stick with them long enough. They saw me at functions by Eric's side, kissing him during events, always by him at Imperial gatherings. I accompanied Eric to every single dinner that the Empire threw for its military personnel and, at each one of these events I saw the same commanding officers, colleagues of his, alone.

Nevertheless, they didn't smile and soon, their eyes avoided me altogether. Eric was the only one gazing down at me sadly with longing in his green, lovely eyes. I could always depend on the desire in his stare.

He stepped up to the edge of the booth, leaning over the rails as if he meant to call me over to him. I wanted to go to him, swallow my pride if only for this one night, simply to sit in the commanding booth with all my superiors. I knew I could get away with it. However, I couldn't make myself give in.

This time, he waved to me, but instead of moving over to him, I lowered my eyes and turned my head away. I wondered whether he would come down and force me up to the booth with him. Before I could find out, the lights on the stage came alive. The crowd roared with delight, pushing me among them to get a better view of the show.

Eric's voice was lost in the shouts of the other Imperial officers in the auditorium. I fell forward with the crowd, trying to fight, pushing through millions of hands and bodies, trying to keep them from crushing me. Above in the booth, Eric began to panic. His eyes widening in fear. Fear perhaps that I would be crushed among the crowd of cheering, reckless officers who knew no better. He knew I wasn't used to this kind of excitement, that I had never been in crowds or in a storming rush of people. Under his watchful and protective wing, I had never experienced such a display nor been involved in such an activity.

I had always been by his side; safely watching the real soldiers wrestle with their duties. I was favored from the other officers and I think that was partially why they hated me. I was never given hard labor or heavy responsibilities and duties that would ruin my manicure. Not to say that I wasn't hard-working or that I hated the military. Oh no, I *loved* the military and I wanted to experience martial life and see the galaxy, to be known as more than just another pretty face. I wanted others to realize this.

The crowd settled down and I regained my balance among their sweaty and eager bodies. Eric restrained himself and fell back into the booth. Seeing that I was well, he took his seat reluctantly beside his peers. Commander Armstrong, who sat beside him, laid his hand on his arm to try to calm him as he caught sight of me down among the crowd; he whispered something into my lover's ear. At once, they both gazed down at me, with Eric warmly smiling at me. Armstrong pointed me out to Eric as if he meant to assure him that I was well and would be fine until the event ended. Eric nodded and pursed his lips in response to Armstrong.

I don't know what was said among them, but whatever it was calmed Eric's fears, and once or twice, he glanced over at me before he straightened himself upon his seat and focused on the event now beginning. Armstrong gestured at me, as a smile spread over his tired face and he turned his attention to the stage, away from me.

"Welcome to the Royal Auction!" came the voice from the center of the stage.

I turned immediately, startled by the loud voice overpowering the auditorium.

An announcer appeared, stepping closer to the front of the stage where I could now clearly see him. He was a tall fellow wearing a long velvet cloak and dressed in black trousers with a fancy vest. In addition, he wore several large stone rings on his fingers and a sparkling pendant on the collar of his silk shirt. In one of his hands, he carried a mic, and spoke into it.

"Are you ready, gentlemen?" he hollered into the instrument.

His face was long and not very attractive, but plain and older. He lifted the mic in the air over his head as the crowd roared and their shouts rang in my ears.

"Well then, let's get started, shall we?" he smirked and turned as the velvet curtain behind him opened.

Standing on the edge of the stage were a line of Companions with their eyes lowered and their hands clasped on the backs of their necks, all dressed in royal blue. Their robes partially revealed their pale and hairless muscular chests and arms. Their long hair draped over their shoulders, with the curled ends decorated in glitter.

My heart exploded when I saw them standing there, not far from me. Then the same desire overcame me, I felt the pleasure invade my veins and I searched for the one that had stolen my heart upon that stage, but I couldn't find him. *What had become of him?*

Again, the announcer extended his hand out to greet the crowd of Imperial officers. Just then, a scholar raced onto the stage and whispered something into his ear. The crowd fell silent, then the announcer turned back as a smile spread upon his eerie, long face. He gazed into the faces of millions with delightful news.

"I've just been informed that Supreme Admiral Patrick is now joining us up in the commanding booth!"

The crowd glanced back, and just as the announcer had indicated, the Admiral appeared, led into the booth along with two other officers; one an unknown younger officer, while the other was Admiral Lauren, commanding officer for Station Delta.

As I caught sight of the Supreme Admiral, he was greeted by the other commanding officers sitting near him. They rose to salute him then took to their seats. The admiral then greeted the crowd with a single gesture of his hand and took his seat. The announcer bowed as the crowd of Imperial officers below saluted the Admiral properly. I stood up straight – what an honor this was indeed!

Admiral Lauren and the unknown officer took their seats beside Supreme Admiral Patrick. I didn't recognize the younger officer, but to me, he seemed to be an escort assigned to guide the Admiral upon the decks of Station Victoria. Gee, what an honor that would be, if only it had been me.

Admiral Patrick sat back and gave the event his entire attention. Focused, he folded his hands on his lap, and rubbed the bottom of his chin, consumed with his own thoughts. There was no officer's cap to cover his soft, ash brown locks, and though beautiful, his expression seemed cold and emotionless.

I couldn't help myself; I couldn't help staring up at him with such an emotional feeling coursing through me. I respected him greatly—he was an inspiration to me, not just professionally, but in the very life he lived. Not many could say they knew the Admiral, not many could say they were close friends with him, in fact, no one could say that at all. He was a private and very personal man who preferred his privacy to companionship. Although the rumor was he had made an exception with the Prince and no one seemed to compare to his Highness's affections.

"And now, without further interruptions, let's get started! First up!" the voice of the announcer shouted from upon the stage as the first batch of beauties was brought forward to the center of the stage.

Admiral Patrick settled back in his seat. I was still looking up at him as he adjusted himself. Then he glanced in my direction—he was looking down at me from the booth! Only for a moment, he gazed at me as, again, he rubbed the bottom of his chin in thought, then, crossing his legs, he turned away. Did this mean something? What were the odds of that happening—of Admiral Patrick looking directly at me?

I turned slowly away with disbelief upon my face as a smile spread over my lips. In slow motion, I gazed up at the stage as the first beauty made his way closer and stood right in front of millions of shouting Imperial officers who wanted a chance to purchase this wonder.

This Companion was a lovely blond, with large gray eyes. His long locks danced off his muscular shoulders, and those arms were incredibly thick and strong. He had a boyish face and was as tall as he was well-built. His display brought the commanding officers to attention and the crowd continued to shout and whistle with approval.

"Now, this beauty is a prize if you're interested! Very strong arms and such a beautiful face!" The announcer twisted the blond curls around his fingers playfully.

He then pulled down the robe and exposed the muscular features beneath. He stroked the beauty's bare chest, running his fingers over the features of it. He gripped his waistline, suddenly glancing back at the audience who, with *awe* clung to the movements of the announcer's hands. Throughout the ordeal, the beautiful creature kept his eyes lowered with what seemed to be a tiny smile upon his gorgeous lips.

Still holding the mic in his hands, the announcer smiled and pulled off the cloth from around the beauty's waist, revealing the creature's muscular legs and hardened organ concealed beneath a thong. He then caressed the beauty's cheek. Coming around from behind him, he brought his hand around and placed it on the beauty's leg, stroking his fingers down slowly. The young beauty seemed to blush as he appeared to be instructed by the announcer. He gasped, lifting his head upward as if in ecstasy. Then he lowered his face down again and gazed at the crowd with a devilish smile that was both divine and arousing.

The crowd loved it. They responded with cries of excitement and whispers and whistles.

"I bid 1,000!" came a shout from the booth.

At once, the crowd fell silent as faces turned to see who had given the first bid of the day. Above me in the booth, Commander Armstrong had practically jumped out of his seat to make his first bid.

"I bid 1,000!" he shouted again, this time over the silence of the auditorium.

The announcer came from behind the Companion, squinting his eyes to look up at the commander through the bright lights beaming down over him.

"Sir? We haven't started the bids yet."

Again, there was some silence as the commander took his time to think about the response from the stage.

"Oh, sorry," he uttered, foolishly embarrassed by his sudden outburst.

He seemed to stir in his seat, grinning stupidly in apology to the crowd and his colleagues beside him while shrugging his shoulders.

Once again, the announcer continued.

"We will now start taking bids."

He seemed to be talking directly to Armstrong. The commander rose, waving his hand in the air as if to remind the announcer of his first bid. The announcer nodded politely then directed his attention to the surrounding crowd as the commander took his seat, quite satisfied with his bid of 1,000.

"Okay, then we have the bid of 1,000 from Commander Armstrong. Do I hear 2,000? Anyone?"

The commander grinned proudly again and fell

comfortably back in his chair. Surely, he didn't think there would be *no* other bids? We hadn't even begun the serious bids yet.

There was some silence, then came another shout from the booth on the opposite side.

"2,000!" a commander named Anderson said without further hesitation.

The announcer quickly turned to acknowledge his bid with a grin of approval.

"2,000 from Commander Anderson!" the announcer repeated over the mic.

There was laughter among the commanding officers, as there were whispers. Armstrong sat up in his seat and turned his head around to challenge Anderson's glance.

"Do I hear 3,000?"

Armstrong rose from his seat angrily, lifting his hand to get the attention of the announcer, who seemed to be waiting for his response.

"3,000!" shouted Armstrong, biting his lips with frustration in response to Anderson's bid.

He then slumped into his seat, nodding his head and crossing his arms. Again, there was silence in the auditorium with the exception of the commanding officers' laughter.

Anderson seemed to be trying to avoid Armstrong's stares and comments. He sat comfortably in his chair and appeared expressionless, there was no urgency in the sound of his voice. He was calm and his manners were as dry as Admiral Patrick's, simple and bold, as well as direct.

Again, there was some laughter among the commanding officers in the panel. Commander Armstrong sat on the edge of his chair, looking back at his opponent as if daring him to answer once more.

"4,000? Anyone?" The announcer questioned the two men, then the entire audience.

The crowd seemed to be waiting for either commander's response, then fell into whispers and, once again, silent laughter.

"5,000!" came the response of Commander Anderson, suddenly as bold and dry as before. The crowd fell silent once more.

"5,000 from Commander Anderson!" the announcer shouted over the mic, the audience stirred.

"Do I hear 6,000? Commander Armstrong?"

Again, there was silence then whispers and muffled laughter erupted from among the panel of commanding officers. Armstrong seemed to adjust himself in his seat, nervously trying to make up his mind on what to do next. He grunted furiously, then seemed to rise but fell back onto his seat angrily, consumed by thoughts of defeat.

"Sir?" the announcer asked, wondering whether Armstrong would continue.

Armstrong grunted again, crossing his arms, then waved the announcer away. Defeated at last, he glared over at Anderson with a frown. Anderson, in return, grinned back at him with a nod at his obvious victory, and again a rush of whispers broke the silence, then finally applause.

"Commander Anderson, you are now the proud owner of Royal Companion Victor!"

The announcer bowed to Commander Anderson. Anderson stood as his colleagues rose and applauded him. He took a bow before the panel. It seemed Armstrong was the only one foolishly looking away, still bitter in his defeat. He sat with his arms crossed and a big frown on his tired face.

I looked over at Admiral Patrick—he seemed unmoved by the whole display. Even in this period of entertainment, he seemed uninterested and focused on other matters brewing in his hard and troubled mind. His only acknowledgment to Anderson was a small and simple nod of approval, which Anderson and those around him took as respect enough coming from him. The Admiral's expression remained firm and unemotional. He sat up straight, a gentleman handsomely vacant and dry. His demeanor struck me as cold and the expressions on his face said he could be doing more important things with his time.

I wondered what preoccupied him, as he sat there consumed by his thoughts, among all those rebels, among all these low-lives of the Empire. He seemed bored, watching the time, ignoring all the noise and gossiping, even on the panel not far away from him. Had he no friends to speak with? No others to say a single word to? Had he chosen this life? Or had superiority included this one downfall?

Companion Victor was taken away by the scholars, dragged to the back to be prepared for the commander. The auction continued as immediately the next man was brought up. He was a young Companion who actually seemed too young for the auction but, nevertheless, was brought to the center and displayed by the scholars for the shouting Imperial officers below.

This Companion was a prize for whoever was able to snatch him up. Companions this young, were hardly ever auctioned, but when one was brought forward, usually the response was incredible. Everyone wanted to get his or her hands on one. He was unlike the other Companions, in the sexual sense; he was merely too young, but a trophy no less. He appeared to be the tender age of 18.

"Here's a beauty, a young one in training. He's intelligent and well-educated. You'll be happy to know this little creature once kept Prince Seth company before he was brought here for re-education." The announcer smirked, playfully winking at the audience, aware of what such information would do.

"Okay then, who would like to begin the bids?"

Re-education usually meant education to be a Royal Companion. Which wasn't bad, just that he was still young and probably an orphan. To be approved for Companionship, you had to be honored by one of the Royals with this pleasure; as in this young man's case, being a Companion to Prince Seth had surely brought him great approval.

Just as before, Armstrong rose again, but although he almost leapt out of his seat, it was an officer in the back whose voice was heard answering first, before he had the chance to speak.

"1,000!" yelled the young officer sitting next to Admiral Patrick. It seemed the Admiral had ordered the officer to answer and begin the bid.

Armstrong spun around, his eyes were wide open, and his sweaty face was turning red with anger at the challenger. He seemed to growl at the young officer who was standing beside the Admiral. The young officer fearfully shrank back, overtaken by the commander's threatening form as he nervously took his seat beside the Admiral.

Armstrong eyed Admiral Patrick wickedly. The Admiral seemed to ignore his glance altogether and adjusted himself upon his seat, resting his head on his hand.

"Ah, Admiral, may I add what a good choice!" the announcer remarked.

The Admiral pressed his lips back. No expression fell over his face as he nodded his head.

Still, Armstrong rose and stood up within the panel, extending his hand out to catch the announcer's attention. For a moment, I thought the announcer was simply ignoring further bids, but who could ignore Armstrong? He waved his hand in the air, again bringing laughter among the panel of commanding officers, but he had no shame.

"Excuse me! I bid 2,000!"

The announcer turned very slowly, holding the mic close to his mouth as if he had merely missed the commander. Acknowledging him now, he nodded in response to his bid of 2,000.

"3,000!" The young officer once again stood, even before the announcer could pronounce Armstrong's bid.

"4,000!" At once, Armstrong glared angrily back at the officer challenging him.

The Admiral flashed Armstrong a frown—the first expression I had witnessed coming from him.

Immediately, the Admiral sat up and pulled the young officer down to his side. Armstrong looked nervous. Still, he stood his ground as he saw the Admiral whisper into the officer's ear before he fell back into his seat with the same scowl on his face. The Admiral's young escort appeared nervous, and in a shaky voice, after clearing his throat, he once again spoke up.

"6,000!"

Surely the commander would not challenge the Admiral. The crowd fell silent, there was no laughter this time, just soft whispering around the panel as the officers and the announcer waited. But yet again, the commander stood his ground bravely.

"7,000!" shouted the commander without hesitation.

The frown on the Admiral's face hardened as it seemed his patience was reduced. He pulled the young escort to his side once again. The other commanding officers in the panel were either encouraging the commander or advising him to quit aggravating the Admiral before he got himself into hot water. Armstrong waved their concerns away with a foolish smirk and even a small chuckle to add to the Admiral's frustration.

Once again, the young officer speaking for the Admiral answered the commander, rising from his seat with a sense of victory in his voice, not like before. I could surely understand the pride running through his veins, all the while knowing he was standing beside a well-respected man like the Admiral. I think I would have acted in the same manner.

"10,000!" Everyone gasped and the silence again turned into whispers.

I thought the commander would immediately return with a response, but he hesitated. Though he gazed down at the intense youth upon the stage, he ground his teeth as his lips drooped sadly in dismay. He looked to his colleagues, his closest companions, and friends sitting beside him, like Simpson and my lover, Eric, for advice and comfort. But they had none to give him.

"10,000? Do we hear any more bids? Do I hear 11,000? Commander Armstrong?"

Defeated once again, Armstrong fell back in his seat and threw his arms into his lap in frustration. He waved the announcer's questions away and slumped back in his seat with his arms crossed.

"Shit!" he muttered under his breath as his friends comforted him with words of encouragement. The auction was not finished yet and he didn't have to leave empty-handed. Their words did very little to cheer him up.

"Sold to Supreme Admiral Patrick—Sir, you are now the proud owner of Royal Companion Lawrence, better known as Claiborne. Mind you, Prince Seth might return for him...So, you might get a visit from His Highness." That seemed to bring a smile to the Admiral's face.

The Admiral rose as he accepted the applause of the crowd of Imperial officers. His expression had regained its superiority. The applause faded as the Admiral took his seat. Poor Armstrong, twice he had been badly defeated by his colleagues, robbed of his chances for companionship.

Royal Companion Lawrence was led away from the stage by the scholars to be prepared for Admiral Patrick. The rest of the show continued without incident. Other Companions were sold, and some awarded to ordinary Imperial officers for great achievement on duty. I could have been one of those, if only I had taken the offer. There were two other individuals besides myself, that had been announced on stage and handed their trophies.

Then came the moment I had been waiting for, except there would be nothing I could possibly do. It seemed he was the highlight of the show. When they brought him out, he was dressed in a red robe and he immediately got great applause from everyone. Yet, I noticed Admiral Patrick rise from his seat and exit the panel with his escort by his side.

The announcer continued in the same manner, displaying the Companion, removing the cloak from him and exposing his muscular chest and lovely features to the audience. He pulled off the cloth as he had with the previous companions to reveal the hardened muscle throbbing between his well-toned legs. He made the Companion turn slowly, and as he did so, the Companion lifted his arms and extended them out before him. His head dropped back as he closed his eyes and a gasp fell from his lips. His long, beautiful hair fell over his backside, swaying on the exposed buttocks behind the red thong.

THE ANNOUNCER CAME BACK AROUND and, with his hand, spanked the bare rump several times, bringing the audience to their feet, cheering. Immediately, the auditorium soared with shouts. Commanding officers leapt to their feet, calling out their bids over one another.

"One at a time, gentlemen!" the announcer smirked. "Please!"

The announcer then ordered the red-haired beauty to turn back around so that he faced the crowd, then made him kneel beside him, ordering him to bow his head. The beauty did as he was told, dipping before the announcer, kneeling so that his legs parted slightly and those around him were able to see the throbbing shaft between his muscular thighs.

"Yes, go ahead, Commander Simpson! 1,000 yes... Yes sir, Commander Henderson, 2,000?"

"3,000!" came another bid from Commander Thompson.

"3,000, yes!"

"4,000!" Yet another came, interrupting the announcer. He could barely keep up with the crowd from the panel.

"4!" he barely had time to accept the bids when, again, Armstrong stood.

"5,000!"

"5,000 from Commander Armstrong!"

Everyone became silent for a second, turning to glance into Armstrong's eyes for a brief moment, but as fast as they had stopped, the bidding resumed without delay. It seemed they were trying to outbid each other. It was a race without an end.

"6,000, 7,000!" The announcer could barely keep up with the commanders disputing over their bids with one another.

"8,000, 9,000, 10,000, 12, 14,000!"

"I bid 20,000!"

Again, silence fell over the crowd. The commanding officers stared at one another, questioning each other in search of who had announced such a bogus bid.

"20,000 from Admiral Lauren!"

The commanding officers stopped bickering with one another and glared at the Admiral. A smaller gentleman, sitting in the Admirals' area a little higher up in the booth, smiled down at them.

Eric had told me a little about him. In fact, we had had an argument about him while attending an Imperial banquet one evening when I rose to defend this man, I knew nothing about. We were at an Imperial party, and though we were still in uniform, we were free to mingle with the commanding officers of higher rank. I was Eric's guest but not the only boy-toy at this banquet; though there were few among them with a date, fewer without.

"How can you say that? The man is a snob and stuck-up with everyone, with the exceptions of the Royals and Admiral Patrick. But that's no excuse. He has no respect for his fellow officers even in the same rank as himself. And, if you ask me, that's why he is a very lonely person."

"Perhaps," I said, picking up my glass of wine while glaring over to where Lauren sat at the Admirals' table, alone, sipping his glass of wine.

The rest of the Admirals seated at the same table were holding conversations with one another. Some of them had joined the commanding officers' table. Though they were not divided by rank here, they separated themselves from one another. Most commanding officers had friends in other ranks, and those that had none, couldn't even get stuck with their own colleagues in high-ranking positions. And so, Admiral Lauren, was left alone to drown in his sorrows.

"Or maybe he just needs a good spanking and someone to dominate him. It seemed to work on you," I said with a smirk, drinking from my glass. Eric frowned, but I could see him blushing. His jealousy always made him do so.

"Dominated... me?" He smirked this time, almost laughing, but I could sense he knew it was true.

"Oh, so you think you know what he needs?" He turned and glared over at the lonely figure of Lauren, sitting there, sipping his glass of wine.

"I didn't mean it that way. I just think if..." And I hesitated and fell silent, considering the delight of spanking the man.

I think that was my mistake—when allowed, my true desires revealed themselves. I don't even remember what point I was trying to make. But by then, I had already put my foot in my mouth, and it was too late.

"If? I don't believe this!" Eric gulped his wine down quickly and slammed the glass on the table, luckily not breaking it. He raised his eyes at me, silently staring at me as he felt the wine burning his throat.

"You want him? Is that what you're trying to say? It's like a challenge for you, isn't it? Playing mind games!" He had to lower his voice when others began staring at us.

"No! I'm simply saying if..." I fell silent, realizing what trouble revealing my thoughts had gotten me into again.

"If what? If you had your way with him, you could dominate him as you have me!"

"No, that's not what I'm saying! It's nothing like that!"

He froze up, burning inside. He didn't know how to hold his tears back. He had been strong once, a bold and cold form that dominated me. Now he was falling apart and didn't know how to hide it anymore. He was hurting and I could sense it in the way he spoke and the way he looked at me, though he tried to conceal it by turning away. I saw it in his eyes.

"Why must you always become jealous? You don't trust me!" I snapped back.

He grunted, slamming his fist on the table, but then, cold and collected, he restrained himself, straightened his posture, and sat up. The expressions were wiped from his face as he stood up slowly and gazed down at me coldly. Now, this was the commanding officer I had once known; the cold and uncaring master that had once frightened me.

"I have no time for this, do as you will."

He walked out and left me sitting at the table alone. I didn't move, I didn't even turn to watch him leave. I just sat there drinking from my cup. Perhaps I didn't care either, and I smirk when I say that now. Strangely, I knew he would be racing back to my side. He hated talking about his feelings. I was sure I had touched something delicate in him: his pride.

People were staring at me, but soon, their eyes left me and I felt like one of those lonely faces was staring in my direction, trying to catch my eyes, hoping for a quick rendezvous. But the only person's glance I met was that of the Admiral, who was grinning at me while he drank from his glass.

Somehow, he had caught sight of me from across the banquet room and was now gazing at me, hoping I would look right at him. Had he seen Eric here by my side before our argument? Had he known of our relationship? Not that it ever mattered. Not to me, at least.

Admiral Lauren rose slowly from his seat and began to walk over to me. As soon as he stood over me, I could see just how handsome and mature he appeared. The cold nature of his gestures, and even those lines on his face, were genuinely cruel. His eyes glared down at me. A sparkle exploded from the baby blues as a crooked smile spread over his lips. This was the smile, the sinister and cruel smile that only fellow officers had known. I didn't understand how such a devilish smile as this could make me want him more. He introduced himself and invited me back to his chambers. I didn't hesitate for a minute.

———

"Do I hear 21,000? Any more bids?" The announcer's voice broke into my thoughts as I gazed at the red-haired beauty.

"No? Commanders?" questioned the announcer.

There was silence again. The officers took their seats with frowns on their faces, bitter about their defeat.

"Very well, then. Sold to Admiral Lauren for 20,000. Sir, you are now the proud owner of Companion Ivan."

"So, his name was Ivan," I uttered to myself.

"Gentleman, this now concludes our auction! Have a nice day and enjoy!"

The announcer moved back and disappeared through the velvet curtains as they were being closed.

I glanced back up at the booth again and saw Eric's face looking down at me. He waved to me. Ignoring his gesture and hoping to avoid him, I pushed my way through the crowd of officers, as they were leaving the auditorium. But as soon as I tried to do so, I caught sight of the commanding officers, Armstrong and Simpson, at a distance from me in the clearing auditorium. I was being led, along with the lower-ranking officers, in the other direction, in order to allow the commanding officers to get out of the auditorium faster.

Once they caught sight of me, they began walking over in my direction instead. I had no choice but to make my way over to them. I came out of the crowd of officers and stepped over. After saluting, I stood up straight in their presence, wondering what they were up to.

"At ease, Soldier," Armstrong said. He came closer as Simpson lurked in the distance.

I had a sense that Simpson didn't like me much. Eric and he were very close friends. I felt I had come in between their relationship in some way. He revealed his hate for me whenever he had the chance. But Armstrong, on the other hand, always wanted to offer me a place to run to, if I ever needed it. There was never a time he didn't remind me of this; he made it quite obvious that he had a thing for me.

"I want you to talk to Eric," Armstrong whispered softly into my ear as he came closer.

"Sir?"

"I said drop the ranks, at least for this moment, my boy. Call me by my first name, Peter." He wrapped his arm around me and began to walk with me.

"Talk to him. Now, I know this is none of my business, but Eric is a friend of mine. And I hate to see him upset. All I ask of you, my boy, is that you talk to him. Try to work things out between the two of you. He's a good man. And, like I told you before, if there is anything you ever need from me, you just let me know, and don't hesitate to ask. Don't be shy." Armstrong smirked, patting my cheek playfully, and moved aside as we both caught sight of Eric descending the booth steps.

Eric stood there at the bottom of the stairs, looking in my direction. The commanding officers dismissed themselves and hurried out of the auditorium, leaving us alone. Eric walked up to me and immediately embraced me. He held me tightly then gently fell away from me and reached out to touch my cheek. I moved away from him.

"I leave today. And I haven't changed my mind," I simply said, turning to meet his eyes.

He smiled warmly, which was something I didn't expect him to do. He stepped over to my side and placed his hand on my shoulder.

"I knew you wouldn't change your mind," he smirked suddenly. "I'm not going to stop you, Gabriel. I want you to do whatever makes you happy. If leaving Victoria to seek whatever it is you want will make you happy, then do so. I won't stop you. I don't want you to hate me. I love you too much. I can't hold you back from what you want." Again, he touched my cheek and smiled.

I didn't know what to say. I was left amazed by his words—and confused.

"I don't understand..." I uttered foolishly. Perhaps I feared he just didn't care and had stopped loving me. He seemed to almost read my thoughts.

"I thought you didn't want me to leave..." I sadly mumbled, lowering my head.

"I don't, but I can't *stop* you and I hate to see you sad. I want you to be happy. I've already made the appropriate arrangements for you. Commander Armstrong will take you back with him to Delta. He's making a stop at the Station. There, he will take care of further arrangements with the commanding officers that he trusts. That way you won't have any problems or further paperwork to worry about. There's only so much I can do. But you should be okay."

I couldn't believe he had done all this for me. It seemed he had given this a lot of thought. But sadly, it was hard for him to see me go, and I could tell. I fell into his arms and embraced him and moved to kiss him, but he stopped me. I froze, amazed, as he pulled himself away from me. He had never refused a kiss from me before, and now he drew away and stopped my lips from touching his plump mouth. The tension beneath his uniform's pants had hardened, and the desire on his face was obvious. The excitement inside me grew, aroused and hard; a kiss would no longer do.

He seemed to pull himself together, gasping lightly. He removed his officer's cap from his head before he gazed into my eyes again.

"No, not here. Let's go somewhere private. Alone." I smiled, recalling his regulations as I walked away in his arms.

DELTA STATION

I was happy when the shuttle finally landed in Delta's bay. For the entire trip to Delta, Commander Armstrong would not stop telling me all about how he had been passed over for promotions and so forth, thanks to Admiral Patrick. I took it he didn't like the Admiral. He warned me about the other man, he told me to watch my back.

"Don't tell anyone what I told you, and don't get yourself into any trouble with the Admiral. He's like buddy-buddy with the Emperor. God, I can't stand that guy! Anyhow, follow me, Soldier."

We walked down the ramp out of the shuttle. The bay was crowded with pilots either working on their ships or moving about the harbor. I stopped to glance around, taking in the air and the environment that was Delta. This was the famous Station in the depths of space where the Prince molded pilots. Not many knew the Prince was a great pilot and warrior.

"Try to keep up, boy. You're a soldier, so act like one."

"Yes, sir."

"At ease, you don't have to worry with me, but remember where you are and salute your commanding officers."

"Yes, sir, Commander."

Commander Armstrong smirked slightly and began to walk ahead of me as I tried to keep up with his speedy step. The commander was a regular man, not entirely fat, but not entirely thin either. His small, round head was going bald, but the little hair on it concealed his scalp well. His round face was clean-shaven, except for the few dents on his skin from a serious acne problem that seemed to have plagued him in the past. He had an easygoing personality and a mellow voice that was never quite professional, whether he tried or not. At times, he was too comfortable and too laid back—it was hard to believe that he had made it as a commanding officer.

I followed like a lost, tiny puppy with my bag tossed over my shoulder. I tried not to catch the eyes of many, but for some reason, I couldn't seem to avoid questioning glances and stares as we walked down the corridors. Others stopped to whisper, and panic began to rise inside me. Armstrong pulled me closer;

grinning at the many faces staring back at us. I couldn't understand why.

"Try to ignore them. They're just surprised to see you with me. I'm a Big Shot around here, that's why!" He foolishly waved his own comments away when he got no reaction from me, and we continued down the corridor.

We came to stop at an entrance. Immediately, he pushed in a code and the doors parted for us. We entered and the doors closed behind us. I stopped halfway inside and looked around. Armstrong made his way to the bar at the end of the chamber and immediately poured himself a drink. The chamber was fairly large, a reasonable room for a commander—cadets shared their space, while other ranking officers had a more suitable place if favored by handsome commanding officers, as in my case. I was one of the lucky ones.

The place had a second room which looked from a glance like a bedroom. A bar with bar stools and even a small kitchen and sink area formed what appeared to be the living room area. Behind the bar, a medium window revealed the stars of space outside and gave the place a second-class rating compared to what most commanders usually had as a reasonable chamber.

"You can stay here a while; I'll get your paperwork together. It's gonna take some time, but I'm sure

I can pull some strings." He gulped the drink in his hand and refilled it at once.

"Don't worry," he assured me, catching my disappointed glare.

"Can I offer you a drink?"

I shook my head, looking around.

"Go ahead, make yourself comfortable. You can put your things over in that area. Come on, sit and have a drink with me, boy. Don't be shy."

I dropped my bag on the floor and slowly made my way over to him. Even though I had refused a drink, he poured and held one out to me anyway. I took it so as not to be rude.

"Sorry, I don't get many guests." His thin lips smiled at me, the acne on his tired round face had left marks on his cheeks and his thinning hair was graying at the sides. He had handsome features, if only the acne had not scarred him, and in some way, he had the cutest lips, and a small round nose and round chin.

"So, what do you think of Delta so far? Pretty weird, huh? You should see Deco. All that stupid deco architecture! How lame... the Emperor's idea. I personally don't like art deco, what about you?"

I shrugged my shoulders. I didn't even know what art deco looked like.

"Hungry? Sorry, can I offer you something to eat?" I just shook my head and took a sip from the glass in my hand. *Hmm, rum?*

He went around the bar and began searching for something, and pulled out another bottle from under the counter.

"I tell you, I think they rigged that auction. That last one was a real beauty! God that sucks!" he smirked.

He chuckled as he poured himself another glass of brandy. He brought the bottle around. I could already feel the rum hitting my head. I rarely drank hard liquor. I was mostly the wine kind of drinker. Armstrong glanced over at me.

"You okay, boy? Don't tell me that stuff is already hitting you. You're just like Eric, he can't hold his liquor." He began to laugh as he poured yet another drink for himself.

I nodded, feeling my head spinning, then gulped the remaining rum in my glass.

"Whoa! Take it easy, boy! We don't want you to pass out on your first day on duty!" He laughed, but his laughter sounded more like muffled noises inside my head. He took the glass from my hand and handed me another one filled with brandy.

"Here, you'll love this stuff!"

He held me up as I almost fell over. Again, he laughed and took a sip from his glass while he continued talking. It didn't matter if I didn't get to say a word, he kept on speaking. Not that it made sense; I couldn't understand what was happening around me.

His voice sounded muffled, and his laughter echoed in my head.

"Yeah, that was really bad! I didn't even get a chance! Not one! Can you believe that? I tell you, that thing was rigged. But that doesn't mean I have to be alone for the rest of the evening," he mumbled as he downed the drink. Finishing it, he poured himself another.

I gulped mine and clumsily extended my glass for him to refill.

"All right, boy! Drink up, there's plenty of it!"

I started laughing as he poured brandy into my glass, realizing and recalling the event in my mind. Picturing him standing up and waving his hands at every beauty who was brought up on the stage. He gazed at me, smiling foolishly. The ridiculous grin flashed across his mouth and, all at once, I burst into uncontrollable laughter.

"What?" he smirked as I almost collapsed into his arms again.

I made a gesture or two, waved my arms into the air, mimicking him, hoping he'd remember and realize what a crack-up he had appeared at the auction, then laughed deliriously out loud. He started to chuckle along with me, realizing what I was laughing about, remembering him standing there in front of his colleagues and Admiral Patrick. His face turned pink as he managed a small chuckle, choking the drink down.

"What? You think it's funny?" he asked, chugging down the drink, but then he thought about it for a moment and fell into a frenzy of laughter along with me.

"You're right, it is!" He continued to laugh, taking another drink.

"You're a nice person, Sir," I said in my drunken state.

"Call me Peter... My name's Peter."

"Peter. Beautiful name," I mumbled through drunken lips and grinned, drinking once again from my glass.

"You think so?" he asked, smiling tenderly and reaching to touch my cheek.

Distracted, I lost my balance and dropped the glass; I watched it shatter on the floor before me.

"Oops! It's Okay, don't worry," Armstrong assured me. I collapsed into his arms and brushed my lips on his.

Consumed with liquor, I felt drawn to kiss him. I could feel the hardening lump between his thighs pressed against my leg as he fought hard to restrain himself.

"Whoa!"

He immediately set his own glass down on the counter and took a good hold of me. He dragged me into the next room and dropped me on a soft surface. I felt warm all over, my head still spinning, but I felt relaxed and numbed by the liquor in my body.

As I lay there, I opened my eyes and saw Armstrong over me briefly; he was looking down at me, unable to make a decision. He seemed to be spinning along with the room. He came down on me and laid right next to me, then immediately began to kiss my face gently, without further hesitation. I didn't stop him. He came closer, still hesitating, and began to kiss my lips.

"Yes, you like that, my boy? It's all right, I won't hurt you. I just want you. Eric doesn't have to know."

He kissed my lips, pressing his mouth roughly upon mine. I didn't move nor fight him. I couldn't. I felt relaxed with the liquor in my veins. I was his prisoner.

He began to unbutton my uniform jacket and slowly pulled apart the fabric. He devoured the soft skin beneath with his caresses and his lips. He rubbed his hardened pecker against my leg, slowly touching the aroused lump beneath the folds of my pants.

"Oh, Gabriel... if you were mine, I'd give you so much!" He pulled my pants down slowly and began to please the throbbing muscle with his mouth.

I held back; the pleasure coursed throughout my body. I wanted to escape him, and yet, at the same time, I found myself wanting to take him.

I felt his tongue lap the muscle, stroke after stroke, pulling me, sucking the pleasure from me. But I held myself back, as lap after lap brought me closer to ecstasy, feeling that greedy mouth of his eating and swallowing my prick into the regions of his throat and arousing the both of us.

I gasped as I reached to touch his head and felt his mouth swallow the cock and, at the same time, I felt the top of his tongue against the skin, pleasuring me in agonizing delight. A whirlpool of pleasure collapsed over me and I fell into the moment of ecstasy. Nevertheless, he didn't stop until I was moaning and whimpering beneath him.

He rose over me once again. Smiling, he wiped his lips and unzipped his pants slowly, pulling his dick from within his pants. He lifted me to my feet and turned me around, then made me bend in front of him as he drove his shaft into me. I cried out immediately as he pushed hard into me, stroke after stroke, penetrating my anal cavity viciously. He was a rough man. He didn't stop, screaming along with the pleasure cascading from his body.

"Feel me, Gabriel! I know you like this!" He pulled my arms back and held me in that manner, pulling me by them as I rode his prick with roughness. He spanked my buttocks as he continued moving in me!

"Eric is a fucking lucky bastard! He gets to fuck you whenever he wants to. I must admit I've had my eye on you for a while now."

He slowed down as he felt himself reaching the moment of ecstasy.

"Not just yet, I probably won't get another chance like this again."

He stopped, and once the feeling ran through his body, he resumed moving against me. As I cried out, he began to spank my buttocks. I had to admit I was enjoying this.

There came a knock at the door. At once, Armstrong turned, just as a form entered his chamber and stood at the door of the bedroom. He stood there in the darkness, staring back at the figure. Sweat rolled down his plump cheeks as he continued to move into me, never stopping nor giving the visitor the slightest care or concern.

"Commander?" I heard a woman's voice pierce the darkness suddenly.

"God damn! Can't you knock?" Armstrong yelled, only when he realized who it was. It seemed like he recognized the woman.

"Oh, what do we have here?" she hissed, staying at a distance, the darkness concealing her face in the shadows. But it was her firm voice that frightened me and made me tremble slightly.

Armstrong released me. I fell on the bed, face first, as he stood in the dark chamber with his pants over his ankles and the organ jerking wildly beneath his officer's jacket where it was barely concealed.

———

"WHAT DO YOU WANT? Can't you come back when I'm finished? I'm fucking horny as hell!"

"No chance, the Admiral wants us on the bridge immediately."

"The Admiral, here? When?" Armstrong hissed in disbelief.

He couldn't believe his luck, first at the auction, and now here at Delta when he was trying to get laid —once again, the Admiral was interfering.

"Yes, weren't you briefed?" The woman asked, though she didn't sound surprised.

"Shit, I just got back. Oh, what does he want now? I hope he's not upset about that little incident back in Victoria."

"Incident? Hmm, yes, I've heard." She seemed to laugh dryly, but her efforts were a poor attempt to sound amused.

"I guess I saved your ass once again," she hissed with deep resentment.

"Ha! Ha!" Armstrong exclaimed sarcastically, but it seemed her demeanor made him nervous, and he backed down.

"So, I see you won yourself a prize in the auction, after all, Commander?" she said, not sounding the least bit interested.

"No, I didn't! The Admiral beat me to it again!" Armstrong snapped, recalling his rival at the auction mocking him from the Admiral's throne.

"Ah, then who is the boy? He's a beauty, certainly

not your date, is he?" the woman sarcastically said. Again, her laughter sounding phony in an attempt to disguise disgust brewing in her words.

"AND WHY NOT?" Armstrong asked, frowning at her.

"No reason," she chuckled as she came closer for a better examination.

"Please pull your pants up, Commander!" she remarked, not at all impressed with his manhood. And Armstrong knew she'd seen him naked, and it excited him, but no matter what it did to him, it did nothing to her. And he hated that. She was unemotional, like there was not a sexual desire in her body, and he couldn't recall once that he had seen her heated and ready to fuck anyone. What did it take? He wondered now, standing in the dark chamber with his dick hanging out of his pants, horny as hell, and yet she was unresponsive.

———

ARMSTRONG PULLED his pants up and walked over to the shadowy figure by the entrance.

"What did you do? Get him drunk? Is that the only way you could get him to sleep with you?"

"Very funny!" He noticed she didn't laugh, and as he glanced back at me, he answered her.

"Yeah, with brandy and rum."

"Ah tsk, tsk, poor Commander."

"And I was fucking him until you came in here and intruded!"

"Well, the Supreme Admiral is coming! I just thought you might like to know. Besides, you can have him again; I don't think he'll be going anywhere. I'm sure he'll be passed out for some time."

"Indeed. I can hardly wait. I haven't even come yet! God, I'm so fucking frustrated!"

"Sexually frustrated, huh?" She grinned as he adjusted the organ beneath his trousers.

"Ah, fuck this! I need it! One quick one, just for now! Then I'll go."

"Fine. I'll wait outside. Don't take too long. Supreme Admiral Patrick will be waiting in the tower."

ARMSTRONG DIDN'T WAIT for her to leave; he barely paid her attention as he came back to the side of the bed and pulled me by the legs to him at the edge. He lifted me like a fragile rag doll, and as he held me, I wrapped my arms around his neck and kissed his cheek. At first, he resisted my lips, but as he again unzipped his trousers, the muscle beneath came to life between my legs. He began to viciously kiss me, feeling the penis between my thighs. The woman smiled, shaking her head, and disappeared through the entrance of the bedroom, leaving us alone in the chamber.

He forced me to turn from him and rammed his cock into my backside and began riding me wickedly, taking my already hardened organ in his gentle grip and repeatedly stroking it. I gasped as he viciously ripped through my backside, electrified with devilish pleasure, I felt myself released. Weakened, I came to the moment of ecstasy once more. Armstrong didn't stop, he was still moving in me, his cries became louder as he finally climaxed.

He pulled me closer, wrapping an arm around me to hold me against him as he continued to move savagely into me. I felt his buttocks rapidly moving, the muscles hardening and flexing as he shifted, gasping and panting as he did so. He moved his hands over my waist, held me in that manner, moving my waistline against the muscle until the pleasure was achieved. He huffed one final gasp, then cried out. Within seconds, I felt the warmth of his manly juices gently run down the back of my leg.

"Damn! That was the best fuck I've had in a long time!"

Those were the first words that escaped his foul mouth. Like I had said, there's nothing professional about him at all. He released me, gently pushing me from him. I fell on the bed, rolling on my back and barely caught sight of him looking down at me while he wiped his dick clean and pulled his pants up.

He bent over me and reached out to caress my pecker as it hardened against the side of my leg. The muscle jerked at his touch, suddenly awakened. At this, he grinned with delight and moved back.

"Get some rest, my boy. As soon as I come back, we're gonna have some more fun."

The last thing I saw was his plump ruby face burning with passion, and those lips tucked back as he seemed to conceal his excitement by biting them. He walked to the door and, taking one last look over at me, edged towards the exit and disappeared from the chamber.

All the pent-up frustration, the boredom that had lately haunted me while I was with the oh so loving Commander Armstrong had dissipated. I was utterly, physically satisfied. Curling into a ball, I wrapped the silk sheets over my naked buttocks, and though I made attempts to remove the officer's jacket, I couldn't even sit up any longer. So, with a satiated sigh, I closed my eyes and fell into a deep sleep...

THE ESCORTS

THE AFTER

A male voice whispered into my ear. Delicate, soft hands reached to pull me up.

"Eric?" I muttered as the sweet fragrance of citrus, vanilla, and something floral reached my nostrils. It seemed too feminine for a man to wear, but I would often use such lovely scents on myself to invite or entice.

"I need to get you out of here. But you'll need to help me," he whispered pressing his lips against my cheek. His lips were warm and soft, smelling of strawberry lip balm. He draped my arm over his shoulder.

It was difficult opening my eyes; they hurt whenever I attempted to. Everything was hazy; I couldn't see the man. Nor could I remember where I was. It was hard putting the pieces of this nightmare together. "Where am I?" I uttered.

"Somewhere you do not want to be." He had a soft and gentle voice. He seemed almost timid, but I could sense that he wasn't.

We started moving. My feet dragged at first, trying to gain a step. My lips and throat were dry, then the pain between the bridge of my eyes started throbbing horribly. The lights were bright, but weren't the lights in the corridors always this way? *Shit!* I had a sinking suspicion I was walking down the same corridor as commanding officers and Imperial officers did to get to their quarters.

"Come on; you have to help me," he said.

"Who are you?"

"Let's worry about that later. First, let's get out of here before the commander returns."

I don't know what happened after I felt my legs moving. His voice whispered into my ear before I felt the soft surface of fresh sheets and a pillow hit my face. There was that sweet scent of cinnamon and vanilla upon the bed, perfume perhaps?

I thought I heard Eric's voice complaining about running late as he kissed my cheek. I shooed him away.

"Let me sleep, Eric," I grumbled.

"Gabe, you need to get up. You'll be late. You know how superior officers are about tardiness."

Gabe... Now, there was a name I hadn't heard in a long time.

"I have nothing to worry about, that's what I have you for."

Eric chuckled.

God, I missed that. The sound of his sweet, beautiful laughter. It was always nice hearing it in the morning.

Someone pushed at my side.

"Eric, stop!" I groaned.

It got quiet...

"Gabriel, you were fun last night." The voice was no longer Eric's, and at first, I didn't recognize it.

"Ready for round two, my lad?" *Armstrong?* He laughed.

I pulled away from his touch—wrestled myself away—as sweaty hands reached and touched me. Instead of the touch I knew was there, I felt a soft hand caress the side of my cheek.

"Shh," his voice whispered. "It's all right; you're safe." I felt his gentle caress on the top of my forehead as the locks of my hair were pushed back.

———

I SETTLED INTO THE SHEETS. Eric was beside me in the bed; I could feel it was him—the scent of his cologne invaded my nose. It was a scent I missed so much. He wore it only when he was with me, when he wasn't on duty. It calmed me as his delicate hands and soft fingertips worked over my shoulders. I pressed my face against the sheets. *Oh, Eric!* he always knew how to ease my nerves.

"You're tense this evening."

"It's work," I mumbled with my lips and face pressed against the bedding.

There was a long pause. His hands were the only indication that he was still on the bed beside me. I sensed him pull his hands back and sit up.

"When where you going to tell me, Gabe?" I rolled to my side. He was seated on the side of the bed. He had his hand over his face.

*Oh, shit...*all sorts of things raced into my mind.

He turned his head toward me. For a moment, the confusion was all over my face. Suddenly, I realized what he was talking about.

"Eric, it's just a trip."

"A trip without me? We always take vacations and leave together. Haven't we agreed about going away?"

"You did, not me."

He was pained by my words. "What do you mean?"

I got up, started getting dressed, and grabbed my things.

"Gabe?" He grabbed my arm to stop me.

"What's going on with you? Talk to me."

"I need time," I admitted.

He looked perplexed, unsure of what that meant.

"You need time from what?" his voice asked, fading softly.

"I need time from us."

"Gabe?"

————

IT SEEMED like a century before I awoke. What a horrible dream... The last image of Armstrong's round face barreling over me was too much. My body ached all over. I opened my eyes; the silk sheets felt good against my body. I wrapped them around me to breathe in their perfume. I lay still, listening to the tranquility of the chamber. There was only silence around me. My breath escaped my tired body as I gazed up at the ceiling. I realized I didn't recognize where I was. I listened carefully for the sound of the Commander's voice.

I sat up. There was a young man sitting across from the bed holding a data tablet. He seemed busy checking the device. I didn't think he saw me until I heard him speak.

"I thought you'd never wake," he said without looking up from the device.

"Where am I?" I asked.

"Relax, you're in a safe place." His beautiful golden-brown eyes sparkled over at me as he rose and put the device on the table nearby. He couldn't be any older than 25. Dark strands of hair fell against the peach tone of his flawless face. I didn't recognize the dark maroon uniform he wore.

I felt a little embarrassed to be in his gorgeous presence and look the way I did. I was dressed, but wasn't sure how that had happened. The confusion in my eyes added to the overall look on my face.

He came to sit by the side of the bed. "Do you remember what happened?" he asked.

I tried to put the pieces of what had occurred together in my mind. Random images came to haunt me and those that I did recall, I didn't want to remember.

"Oh, shit," I uttered. I wanted to hurl. I got up putting a hand over my mouth.

He rose to usher me in the direction of the facilities. Before I could lower myself completely down, I dumped the contents of my stomach right into the toilet. It wouldn't stop. Violent contractions came from the center of my gut. The bitter fluid of my stomach acid found its way into my throat and mouth. A burning sensation made me gag. I tried to control it, but once it was going there was no stopping it. Finally, it was done.

I dropped near the toilet. My handsome, unsuspecting caretaker stood at the entrance concern.

"Are you all right?" he asked as he knelt beside me.

I threw him a look—one I'd often given Eric when he asked a stupid question like that.

"Does it look like I'm all right?" I said wiping at the bile on the side of my lip. "What the hell did I drink?"

He helped me up from the floor. If I wasn't embarrassed with my appearance before, I was now. Bile and stomach acid stained my uniform.

"Rum, it's one of the Commander's favorite drinks. The guy is a serious alcoholic. Now there's a man with a problem." He chuckled in such a lovely way that if I weren't such a mess and bitter company, I would have engaged in the delightful laughter.

He helped me clean up before grabbing a cup from one of the compartments on the large spacious counter. He filled the glass with water, then handed it over to me. "Here."

I took it, gurgled it in my mouth for a few seconds, then spat it out.

His fingers stroked the glass of the mirror and brought up a display of blue controls and commands. He pressed a few instructions and selections. A few random screens lit up and a peaceful forest backdrop appeared over most of the mirror's glass. A melody consisting of piano and violins filled the void of silence and awkwardness.

"There we go," he said.

I doubted the music and background was going to

make me feel any better. Reality was starting to sink in.

He moved into an extended part of the bathroom and returned with a single white hand towel. He placed it under the running faucet, then wiped at my uniform. After, he set it down and helped me back to the side of the bed where I dropped like a pile of rocks.

"Oh shit..." I uttered, blinking. My head was aching and spinning once more, and my throat was burning. There was a disgusting taste in my mouth I couldn't get rid of.

"Are things clear now? Do you remember?" he asked sympathetically. There was also a hint of sarcasm to his tone.

"Hardly, bits and pieces. I don't think I really want to remember the rest..." I sat in utter disgust, hoping the taste in my mouth would not make me hurl again.

"Did we—?" I asked while gazing up at him and turning a light shade of red. He knew immediately what I meant. Did I have to ask? I already knew the answer to that question even though I wanted to deny it to some foolish part of myself.

"Have sex with him? Yep. More than once, I believe. He likes them young, and boy, do you fit the bill. Right down to the light tan bod and blond locks." He nodded, pressing his lips together. He examined me; I covered myself when his eyes took a moment to soak me in. I was far more disturbed by my vulnerability; this was something I never thought would happen to me. I was careless, yes, but he was my superior and what he had done...well... that was just wrong.

"That asshole! He took—" The anger took a toll on me before anything else. I didn't want to show I was weak. I stopped and put my hands over my face. My head was still spinning. My reluctant caretaker took a seat on the side of the bed.

"I'm sorry. I know how you must be feeling."

I doubted it. There was a moment of awkward silence between us.

"You're well-groomed for an officer," he said.

I wasn't even listening to him anymore. "What am I going to tell Eric?" I uttered; everything was coming into perspective. Some of the things that had taken place before I blacked out were finding their way into my mind. Embarrassment was there, but I was far angrier. I trusted a man like Commander Armstrong. From the moment we had met—his longing looks, his smiles and stares—had been aimed at one thing: to get me into bed. Well, mission accomplished. I wanted to beat myself up.

I mentioned that concern to Eric, who brushed it off as part of my vain, arrogant, boyish charm. I guess I couldn't blame him for thinking so.

———

"I'M SERIOUS, the man has a thing for me!" I voiced.

"Armstrong is harmless," he argued. "So, what if he looks at you? The man hasn't had a date in years. Besides, why wouldn't he stare at my boyfriend? You're obviously very handsome." He sounded proud of that fact. He was not at all concerned his colleague and close friend Commander Armstrong was eye-fucking his boyfriend.

———

"HEY, IT'S OKAY." The young officer kindly offered his sympathy. I glanced over at him, realizing again he was there.

"So, that explains your well-groomed appearance and manicure. You have a boyfriend. Is he a high-ranking officer?"

I glanced over at him suspiciously. I'll admit, I was curious. What were his motives? Did he want something in return? Who was he, and why did he care?

"Who are you?" I asked warily.

He smiled, which didn't make me feel any less cautious. "Aiden Hoffman. Assistant officer to Captain Periz," he answered. His lovely gaze momentarily fell on me. He looked genuinely sympathetic. "I'm what you call a Companion, but more along the lines of —"

Cutting him off, I immediately asked, "You're an escort?"

He politely smiled. "Most prefer the term consort. Only officers use the word escort." Officers did, because that's what it was, whatever else they wanted to call it.

"They're just like the *exotics*," I sternly said, slightly jealous over what he had revealed.

"No, consorts are picked and must display a list of qualities. For instance: intelligence, beauty, youth, and the willingness to make conversation. Consorts are social companions or Imperial official companions, slightly different then the lovely royal Companions and nothing like the *Exotics*, who are picked mainly for their sexual pleasure." He shot me a look as if to say *I don't do that.* "Royal Companions aren't Imperial officers. Anyone can be a consort. All Royal Companions have royal blood or are from wealthy families. Consorts are not. A consort must always be quick on their feet, remember names. That's a tough one; don't know how many times I had to give Captain Periz the titles of high-ranking Imperial officers. It's important that a consort always remembers certain things for their official."

I grunted; I knew what they were. I didn't need a lecture from him on the descriptions of Royal Companions, consorts or even exotics. I wanted to be one, a right hand to a high-ranking official—I wanted to be his hands, his eyes—but not just to any official; I wanted to be consort to Admiral Patrick.

"Yes, I know what that is," I said. I wanted to pick his mind. I knew hearing the stories of his duties among high-ranking Imperial officers would make me far more jealous.

"To answer your previous question. Yes, I do have a boyfriend, and he's a high-ranking commander," I said very proudly. "Well, *had*, once he finds out about this... Shit! Shit! I should have known better." I glared over at him, moving aside.

Why was he was telling me all this? And why was I revealing anything to him? I knew nothing about him. Hadn't that been the way Armstrong had taken advantage of me in the first place? I had trusted the wrong person.

"Why am I telling you all this? I don't even know you, Aiden." I liked the way his name came from my mouth. There was something angelic about him. The dark uniform brought out the color of his lovely complexion, giving the soft black locks of his hair a glowing shine.

"Because I don't like Commander Armstrong," he stated. The creases of his furrowed brows made him look rather charming. Angry didn't fit his innocent, youthful face. "And what he did to you? You don't deserve what happened to you. It's not the first time he's done this."

Somehow, that didn't surprise me. That guy got

around. Why hadn't someone already put him in his place? The look on my face must have asked that very question. Aiden seemed far more sympathetic.

"How could he get away with this?"

"Believe me," Aiden began, "he's gotten away with far worse."

"Far worse?" I uttered. "I won't stand for this." I angrily voiced.

Aiden put a finger over his own lips to hush me. He looked around, which made me wonder whether or not we were alone.

"You have to forget this, all of it."

"Forget? Are you insane? I'm reporting this! Eric has to believe me now," I uttered in confusion. "Shit... Eric! How am I going to explain this to him? He'll never forgive me. He'll never believe it wasn't my fault." This would destroy him. I cared about him enough to know I fucked up big time.

"Listen to me, Gabriel." He took my hands into his. I felt the softness of his fingers caress my palms and froze. Even in this utter confusion his touch calmed me. "Do you remember the woman?"

I blinked I had no idea what he was talking about.

"That woman with him asked to send you on your way, but before I did, I was to do something.... give you something." He said looking pained by what he was revealing to me. These words immediately got my attention.

"What are you talking about? Something? What do you mean—give me what?"

He lifted a tiny vial; it was so tiny if he wasn't sitting right on the end of the bed, I wouldn't have seen what he was holding.

"It's a calming drug used by officers to calm the Companions punished by the Royals, those that end up in the hands of Imperial officers. This one is her interpretation of it."

"What is that?" I asked, glaring at the tiny glass vial in his hands. It was blue in color.

"It's a drug to make you forget," he said sadly.

"Wait! That asshole was going to drug me?!"

"Well, yeah, but it was her idea."

Did that make any difference? They were both in on this. I put my face in my hands. What the hell had I walked into? I couldn't just let this go.

"Her? Who do you mean exactly?" I honestly just wanted to forget it all. I was ashamed by what I had done and knew that my actions would hurt Eric. I knew I had done this before, but this was different. This was someone Eric knew, someone he talked to, and was friends with. I was an asshole. Did it take this to make me realize Eric's feelings and my feelings for him?

"There was a woman that walked in on us while he was..." I recalled, tiny images of what had occurred flashed in my mind. I shook them away, disgusted with myself.

"Did she sound emotionless?" His blue eyes gently gazed back at me.

"Cold, yeah... Hard as ass, and careless."

"That would be Periz Zandie. Captain Periz. She's in charge of the control deck on Zec. She and Commander Armstrong hang together."

I pursed my lips as he continued. He put the vial back into his uniform pocket. He rose and walked over to the side table to pick of a glass of water.

"You could use more water." He smiled picking up the glass and handing it to me.

"What does she care if the Commander gets in trouble?"

"Drink, you need something other than rum inside you." I saw that tiny smile on his lip. Was he referring to something else rather than rum inside me?

"She usually doesn't. But I suspect she wants something from the Commander. That would be the only reason she's protecting his ass. She only cares about herself...."

"Lucky me, I had to walk into their drama."

Aiden chuckled; he sounded quite charming. If I wasn't in this awful situation, I may have considered him a close friend.

———

Waiting for the strength to find its way back into my limbs I lay back on the bed. Picturing the wires that ran behind the wall. Carrying conversations, video streams, electricity, and more throughout the Station. The same way the currents of pleasure that moved through my limbs when a skilled lover made use of my body. Well, I supposed the lover would not even have to be skilled if I were attracted to them, but that lover wasn't Armstrong. Looking over at Aiden's back, realizing that he was there to babysit me was an uncomfortable thought.

My mind floated back to Eric, and I banished him away. How could I think about him when I was lying in another man's bed, still sticky with his come? He wouldn't understand. My arms stretched over my head, wondering what Armstrong hoped to gain by having tricked me into his bed. Did he have some other quirk? Sex wasn't exactly a mystery to me.

Slowly I sat up, feeling the soreness in my body. Giving away into it, I let the pain wash over me allowing sparks of the memories once again. My fingers drifted between my legs. Aiden was turning back towards me and I let my hand drop away.

"Am I allowed to shower?" I asked him. He shrugged.

"If that's what you want to do. It's definitely nicer than what we have in the cadet quarters."

Rising I walked gingerly towards the bathroom in the mystery quarters. The light flipped on when I entered, and I raised an eyebrow. It was far more luxurious than my own, however, I supposed that was to be expected. He was a Commander. And I was nothing more than his toy right now. If Armstrong had a secret room where he dumped his drugged liaisons, I guess it might as well be comfortable. The large expanse of granite countertop glistened. A bathtub beckoned on one side and I considered lounging around in hot water. Maybe he would respond to some of the requests that flitted through my brain. I hadn't forgotten. That could possibly be used against him at the right moment.

Glancing sideways at myself in the mirror, I couldn't blame him for wanting me. Eric would have said the same thing. I would fuck me in a heartbeat, multiple ways.

Foregoing the tub, I walked over to the standing shower and turned on the tap. The water came to life immediately, steaming within seconds. I pulled off the officer uniform. A sticky mess of man juice and bile covered the outside of the jacket. Climbing into the stream and allowed the pressure pound on my sore shoulders. I could linger under it all day. My fingers ran through the strands of my hair, making a grab for the soap I squeezed it until it foamed in my palm. The scent of bergamot and black pepper arose. It was very different from the lavender and sweet citrus I was used to. It was the same scent I'd caught on Armstrong's sweaty collar. This was the same soap that Eric used. The bottle slipped from my fingers and crashed to the floor, filling the steam with even more of the fragrance. I cursed. I was being silly; it was regulation soap, after all.

I bent over to pick it up, wincing a little. Armstrong had been a little rough with me. What was strange was that it had gotten me harder than I'd been in a long time. However, if he wanted a repeat of what we'd just done, I was going to have to rest up a little. I bit the inside of my cheek. The man had been about to drug me and was using me for some nefarious purpose. Just because he was a good fuck shouldn't make me forget that.

My lips pressed as I put the soap back on the ledge. I needed to take my mind off it. Taking a washcloth, I spread the soap on it and began to rub the cloth over my skin. Regulation soap. Perhaps Admiral Patrick used it as well.

My eyes closed and I imagined his hand running the cloth over my chest, belly, between my legs... Handsome and powerful Admiral Patrick caressing every inch of my body. My longings for him exploded. The same Admiral that Commander Armstrong had just gone to meet with.

I pictured him as I'd last seen him, in the crisp uniform, undressing him in my mind's eye. Each machine-pressed fold was worried by my hands or mouth. He was already pressing towards me before I'd even fully stepped out of my trousers, desperate to have me. He wrapped his fingers in my hair and shoved me down, down...

My head met the wall of the shower stall with a thump. I was thrust out of the pleasant fantasy, as I rubbed at my skull. I tried to catch my reflection in the glass through the clear wall of the shower. Hopefully, the mark wasn't enough to linger. I got back to the task at hand, cleaning myself up and turning off the blissfully hot tap. Stepping out I took one of Armstrong's fluffy towels, much finer than what we cadets received, and began to dry the droplets of water. My skin was still sensitive from the after-effects of sex. Reaching out, I cleared the steam off the glass of the mirror and looked at my reflection.

My head tilted, fingering at a spot on my neck. *Damn*, he'd bitten me. Unable to recall when it happened but doubt it had been he who had marked me. Oh well, it wouldn't be like I was the only man in Delta Station with a hickey. It was basically a common occurrence. No one really bothered to hide them. I only hoped that the Admiral wouldn't see it. I didn't want him to get the idea that I *belonged* to Armstrong or anyone. There were plenty of men on this station that I would fuck. Especially the Admiral. That man could have me any way he liked.

The mirror began to fog again, obscuring my reflection. I rubbed at my hair with the towel and banished another memory of Eric. It had been such a simple thing. Kissing in the shower to come out and rub each other dry. Kiss some more. I missed that, but

I also couldn't deny I wanted far more than he could give me.

I hated myself.

No wonder I'd gotten bored. He was far too good for me. He needed someone sweet, not wicked. I could see the line of my grin in the mirror. Yes, wicked was a good word. I was certainly debauched right now. My head tilted again, trying to remember more of what happened before I'd fallen asleep and been moved to this location. He'd told me I was a good fuck. Well, that was a given. He'd wanted me again. Yeah, well, we'd see about that.

There was also the creepy woman who thought it perfectly fine for Armstrong to take me when I wasn't in my right senses. She wanted to drug me, so that I wouldn't know anything about my night with Armstrong.

I could feel it a little in my stomach, the hangover. Maybe Aiden could give me something for that. Damn, there wasn't much else coming to me. All I knew was that I was never having rum again.

Wrapping the towel around my waist, I walked back out into the main room. Aiden was still sitting there perched on the end of the bed working on his tablet, once again busy typing commands. When he spotted me, he closed the application to give me his full attention.

"Are there fresh clothes for me?" I didn't really want to go back into the bathroom and get the ones

I'd left on the floor. That was disgusting, and no it wasn't vanity, it was just covered in filth.

"There's a fresh uniform in the closet," he replied.

Dropping the cloth around my hips to the floor I walked over to it. If Aiden wanted to watch me get dressed, he could be my guest. He was probably the one who had dressed me and carried me here, he'd seen all there was to see then.

Making sure everything was in its proper place and secure, I began pulling on the pieces. The Admiral was on deck, after all. I might be the cadet stupid enough to let the Commander seduce him over drinks, but the Admiral was everything to me. I would make a good impression on him. He could take me with him. I could be his and only his. I checked my reflection in the full-length mirror. Yes, perfect as always. The collar even hid the mark that Armstrong had left on me.

"Am I allowed to leave?" I asked, catching Aiden's eye in the mirror.

"I was not given explicit orders that would require you to stay."

"Meaning that you're not technically supposed to let me out?"

"Captain Periz doesn't hold much stock in my cognitive ability. I would likely receive only minor punishment for letting you out." He frowned. "It's not like you can get off Delta Station without his permission, but you have been assigned to his command."

That gave me pause. What did Aiden know that I didn't?

"Honestly, this is more about Captain Periz. Armstrong doesn't mean you any harm, other than his insatiable prick." Aiden wrinkled his nose.

I wasn't sure which part he took offense to—Armstrong's prick or the fact that he thought him insatiable. Well, I guess he might be considering that he was a debaucher of drunk cadets.

"But Captain Periz does mean me harm?" I asked, getting stuck on that part of his statement as I turned it over in my mind.

Aiden tilted his head. "I would never dream of guessing what she wants. It would be a fool's errand."

"So, I'm in one of Armstrong's extra rooms?"

"No, one of hers. Take a right as soon as you go out of the room. Follow the hallway until you get to the mess hall. You'll be able to find your way back from there?" He stood up and walked over to the door on the opposite wall. I nodded.

"Excellent. If anyone asks you what happened last night, tell them you do not remember. If Armstrong brings it up, tell him you do not remember. For your own good, don't let Captain Periz think that you weren't given the drug, or worse, that it didn't work." He stepped into the hallway. I was afraid of those last words he had revealed. What if she did realize that it didn't work or that Aiden hadn't completed her order?

"Wait! Why?" I asked, but it was too late, the door had whooshed shut between us, leaving me standing there like an idiot in the secret quarters of a cold, heartless woman who liked to interrupt good fucks, but worse than that, a woman who wouldn't stop an official from taking advantage of an unconscious young cadet.

I shouldn't be thinking that way at all. It would hurt Eric. Then again, wasn't I already hurting him by being here and not with him? I bit my lip and lifted my chin. There were too many questions. I needed to know more.

I pressed the button on the door and felt relief as it whooshed open and let me out into the hallway. There was a surprising lack of officers milling around and doing various things. What time was it? I tried to catch a glimpse of the time anywhere, but nothing clued me in as to the hour. My internal clock felt disoriented.

The noise of the mess hall grew louder as I approached it. It must have been a meal, but which—breakfast, lunch, dinner? Was it the weekend? The evening when events would be open? No, that couldn't be. I'd arrived in the middle of the week; I'd gotten drunk, and Armstrong didn't waste any time getting me into bed. I told myself I wasn't hurt or bitter about it. I wanted to convince myself of that. I had a job to do; I couldn't begin it with drama. As much as I wanted to make that bastard pay, or rather make the woman pay for what he did to me and what she planned to do to me, I knew that wasn't wise. I wondered if it was over. Would they come after me if I remained? Wasn't it in their best interest if I just left and never returned to Delta? Obviously, they were afraid, wanting to drug me to forget it all.

I wasn't trained for drama. It wasn't a big secret that this kind of thing happened. I guess, I just hated the secrecy of it all.

Pausing outside the door, I gathered my thoughts in my head and tried to put a calm expression on my face. My hands were shaking; I didn't know what I would do. Part of me wanted to strike that man straight across the face for what he did. Guilt gathered in my gut; Eric was the only thing that bothered me about this whole thing. His lovely face kept popping into my thoughts. His magical, dreamy eyes were so innocent. What did he know of the goings-on on this other side of the empire? He must know. However, it seemed I knew far more of the dirty secrets in Delta or any other part of the empire. Maybe there was a part of him that I didn't know. *You're just making excuses,* I told myself.

Inside the mess hall the aroma of mashed potatoes, green beans, roast beef, and grilled chicken invaded my nostrils. Lunch time. Fresh coffee was brewing, and fresh baked bread enriched the surrounding air. One thing I appreciated about the Imperial forces of the Sarvakk was that the Empire took good care of its military personnel.

My stomach growled, desiring food. I got into line with the other Cadets. It was one of the times I was glad that I didn't have a single friend on Delta Station. There wasn't anyone to ask questions that I would have to make up stories to dispel. Still, it was also quite lonely.

HARD LABOR

After feeding myself, I started my day getting my orders from my commanding officer and reporting to the docking bay. My day consisted of manning the docking bay, not on the command post. I had to start from the bottom. It was a dangerous task, a hazardous position. If one wasn't careful, it was easy to get hurt. And it puzzled me who had assigned me to such a position. Then I recognized the signature on the order forms. Captain Periz. I wasn't meant for this manual labor. I was more of a technical officer, yet here I found myself. I witnessed two major accidents; two minor officers had been hurt while preparing one of the fighter aircrafts.

I prayed not to run into the Commander, but I found myself among the ranks. Imperial officers marched in the distance and I caught sight of Armstrong making his way over to us. It didn't surprise me he had found me among the men. Wasn't it Periz that had assigned me this task?

He looked in my direction and smiled. The men stopped what they were doing and lined up for him. He saluted, but it wasn't much of a salute. It made me wonder how he had climbed the ranks so far with his unprofessional mannerisms.

The side of his mouth moved, as if he meant to say something, but he didn't. In fact, the atmosphere between us seemed awkward. When we were dismissed, I politely and courteously bid him a good day. I was trying my best to keep my composure, no matter how much I wanted to unleash my rage. However, before I could leave, I heard his annoying voice.

"Have you heard from Eric? How is he doing?" he asked as if he cared. He had a lot of nerve.

Gathering what little self-strength I had left, I stopped and met his gaze. Standing at alert, he waved away my efforts to salute.

"I haven't, sir." That was the honest truth; I hadn't attempted to make contact with him. I didn't know what to say. My guilt would alone get me in trouble. I would give myself away before I could even think of how to explain what I had done, all the ways I had betrayed him.

"Oh, I spoke to him the other day. Of course, he

asked how you were doing. He's concerned about you, Gabriel. You should give him a call. Men like Eric are a worrisome bunch. But don't worry, I put him at ease. I told him I would be keeping a close eye on you." He gave me a grin.

Shit! Worrisome bunch? There was so much I wanted to say to him in that moment, but I bit my tongue.

"I shall give him a call this evening, Sir," I said, unable to meet his gaze.

He came closer and lifted my chin with his large hand when my eyes lowered. I wanted to avoid him seeing the rage breeding inside me. My eyes said everything my voice couldn't. I *know what you did, asshole.*

"Are you okay? Anything troubling you? You know you can always come to me if you need something. This place can get really lonely. Believe me, I know..."

"I'm fine, Sir." There was no way I would allow him to get me drunk and take advantage of me again.

"You sure?" he persisted, grinning. Did he honestly think his smile would cause me to cave in? I wasn't attracted to him. After having his way with me, he thought his lack of charm would get me into bed again, with his looks alone.

"It's just work. This is not what I'm used to. I'm a technical officer. So, I'm not sure why I've been assigned such a task." However, I knew it was that bitch's idea. That was a sure way of endangering someone's life.

"Ah, I see. Well, I think there was a little shifting in your paperwork when you first arrived, but I can get that corrected for you. That's not gonna be a problem."

"Thank you, Sir. I better go." The next crew of men were coming in for their shifts, and I wanted to head to my quarters and hide from those on board. I was moving to leave, when his voice called to me again and I stopped.

"By the way, lad, there is a dinner... a sort of evening function being held for all the high-ups. I thought that maybe you would like to join me seeing as you know no one here?"

"You mean as your date?"

"Well," he hesitated. He's face said, yes. His words were something else. "More like my company, a guest."

"Of course," I echoed the words.

"It would be beneficial for you to get to know your commanding officers. I can introduce you." Entice me, of course.

I bet you would. I didn't doubt he already had said more to them regarding who I was than he was letting on. That was a disgusting thought. He had a point, though. It would be beneficial to get to meet all the important people that could change my life.

"Think about it. You don't have to make a decision now, but the sooner the better. The function is next week."

Another officer came to interrupt us before I could say anything else. I was thankful for that. Before I could escape, I heard the officer say the name that would keep me lingering nearby.

"Admiral Patrick would like to see you on the control bridge, Sir." When he said that, I looked up toward the commanding deck and was surprised to see the Admiral looking into the landing bay from the command deck. Had he been watching Armstrong this whole time? Or had it been me he watched?

"Can't it wait? I'm in the middle of something."

"Unfortunately, not, Sir. The Admiral wishes to brief all commanding officers on the Prince and Emperor's arrival."

"The Prince? Emperor? Here?" Armstrong uttered as he glanced over at me. There was a different look on his face. It was a moment of weakness he didn't want me to see. It was something I was used to seeing in others, but never thought I would see on him. Fear, respect, love, desire. It was the love that was strange to see and threw me off.

"The Prince will be attending the function, Sir, but it's His Highness, the Emperor, who is stopping by today. That is of utmost importance to the Admiral."

"The Emperor?" Armstrong uttered again. I had heard the stories of the Emperor being a tyrant.

There was one about him sending his young son away, because he feared the boy's red mane. I didn't know the entire details of the story.

Armstrong hurried away, saying nothing else to me. I was happy with that.

———

SETTLING myself in my quarters after duty, I thought about the function. If the Admiral would be there, I would have to plan to attend. This had to be a sign.

As I lay upon the soft cushion of my bed, I heard the sirens and announcement the Emperor had arrived. Only higher wigs and fighter soldiers were to gather at the docking bay and line up to greet the Emperor. I had seen it done before. The officers, commanders, fighters, and control deck officers would take a stand and salute His Highness. Armstrong and the rest of the commanding officers, including Admiral Patrick, would be having their visit with the Emperor.

I had only once set my eyes upon the woman who would be in his company. She was a lovely redhead, who reminded me of the young man in the auction. Strange how I hadn't thought about him until now while thinking of the Emperor's Companion. I wondered what had become of him, and to the young man that the Admiral had won at the auction.

I thought about a lot of things, including the

Prince and the idea that he might attend the function of escorts. I wondered if that was even true.

My body was tired from having to work long hours at the bay. I closed my eyes and drifted to sleep.

THE INVITATION

It was several days after my encounter with Armstrong that I met Aiden again in the central hall. It was where we would gather to show off to the upper brass. I had heard that Admiral Patrick would be through again, but there was Aiden, blocking my view. I sighed and tried to step around him. He held out an arm and caught me across the chest.

"Sorry, I'm not interested," I said. It's not that Aiden couldn't be my type. He had that wiry, clerical look that could be incredibly interesting in bed. That type was often as thorough with their lovemaking as they were with numbers. I glanced up at his warm, golden brown eyes. Warmth was a quality that didn't exist for very many people on this installation. It was about power. Or sex. And sex was the part that was

97

always more interesting to me. Aiden was probably the opposite. Warm eyes, cold hands.

"I'm not offering," he replied with a little quirk in the corner of his mouth.

I nearly smiled back in response. I settled my hand on his wrist and removed his arm from me.

"Then, what do you want? I'm waiting for someone."

He gave me a sly look. I frowned. "Admiral Patrick, perhaps?"

"What of it?"

"Captain Periz," he wrinkled his nose, but continued, "has sent me to offer you some terms. She would like you to be the exclusive Companion to Commander Armstrong. I believe she called you some sort of gift."

"Well, fuck that. In fact, you can tell her these exact words. Tell her to fuck off." I bumped my shoulder against his as I walked through. I really wasn't intending to go back to Armstrong. One and done. The man had played games with me to get me into his bed. That was enough to set me off. What was the deal with his friendship or whatever the hell it was with Captain Periz? She could kiss my ass. I couldn't believe she felt the need to drug me to make me forget. What was the point of all that if she was just going to offer me up to him?

Aiden followed me. I could hear his footsteps

clicking on the metal floor. Tap, tap, tap. It was the rhythm of life. I stopped and turned to him. "Seriously? What part of 'fuck off' is difficult to understand?"

"It's not that. I will communicate your sentiment. However, I thought I would offer you this." He held out a data chip to me. I stared at it for a moment, then I grabbed it, sliding it into my data reader. The invitation floated up onto my screen. It wasn't the usual sort of document that would be traded around the Station. It was filled with a flowy type that I could barely read. My mind didn't really get past two words in the center.

"Admiral Patrick is holding a party?"

"And you've been selected as one of the Companions to attend."

"Thanks."

"You're welcome. Captain Periz was not keen on you receiving that, but I grabbed it off Armstrong's desk when she wasn't looking." He gave me a sly smile and a wink. I gaped at his back and grinned. I was starting to like Aiden more and more. However, it also made me wary of his motives. What were they? After what had happened with Commander Armstrong, I couldn't help feeling concerned about everything and everyone.

The invitation was a boon, considering that hanging around in the common areas didn't give me a single glimpse of the alluring Admiral Patrick. I went back to my room, trying to pick out just the thing to catch the eye of the man of my dreams.

THE MESSAGE

When I arrived back in my room, I was surprised to see a message blinking on my comm system. Messages were rare. I pressed the screen to see who it was, and I felt like my stomach was hollow.

Eric.

Eric had left me a message. I hadn't even tried to call him. I didn't know what to tell him or what to say to him. I was guilty of much more than I could admit to. What if he already knew? What if Armstrong had said something, would he be stupid enough to tell him? He might be, if he thought it helped his chances with me.

I couldn't fathom what he wanted from me. I couldn't have left him under worse circumstances. Hell, I'd practically left the man holding his heart in his hands. Guilt swirled in my chest, but I squashed it. He had said he understood that I was unhappy, and he loved me. When you love something, you let it go. I think that's what he'd said... Or it had been equal to whatever other sentimental nonsense that never really made it through my thick skull.

My finger hovered over the button to erase it before I'd even opened it. Poking at the past was never good. I bit my lip, considering my options. It was always difficult, thinking about Eric. In one moment, I could be bored out of my wits at the thought of our time together, but then there was the memory of his kiss on my brow or the way his fingers would brush the back of my hand. I've heard it said that intimacy is made up of those little moments. I have no idea if that is right, but it does make my chest ache sometimes.

Against my better judgment, I pressed the play button. Eric's face floated up on the screen. At first, I couldn't focus on what he was saying. The image of his face caught me off guard. What's the perfect word to describe Eric? Affable. Yes, that was it. He was affable. Always kind and cute in a sort of puppy dog way. I looked at his slightly crooked nose and lost myself in his features. His words had no meaning until he said, "Admiral Patrick."

I hit the rewind button and forced myself to listen. Eric began: "Gabriel, I know I promised to respect the space that you said you needed. I know that in your heart you did what you thought was best. I'm not calling you to try and win you back, so you can take a breath now."

He knew me too well, I thought.

He continued: "I have heard a rumor about the new position that Admiral Patrick holds involving the Emperor and his court. You know it's no secret that the Emperor has a mistress," he paused.

Of course, who didn't know that?

"And, well, he's appointing a guardian to her, as a safety measure. Admiral Patrick has been appointed with the task of finding the right person until a more permanent guardian can be found. The admiral has been considering a member of the Imperial guard. Nothing is certain, yet.

You might have heard about the strange and dangerous prophecy that exists. There is a dangerous cult that might possibly attempt something on the Emperor's mistress or those in his court." He exhaled deeply. "You know that strange cult that would make the papers at times? They're responsible for kidnapping children in the past. Since I know you are likely to encounter these individuals at some point—perhaps they serve in the Emperor's court or under the Admiral... Well, I want you to keep this in mind. I've sent along some documents that I found pertaining to these people. Please, be careful. I'd hate to read about something happening to you in the news feeds."

The image blinked out and left me with a sort of

hole in my chest. I hadn't heard a thing about any of it. Granted, I didn't overly concern myself with the news feeds; that was for dull people like Aiden and Eric to consider, but was there danger? Would the Admiral be in danger, or was he the cause? Someone in his retinue, perhaps?

These thoughts followed me throughout my evening. For the first time since arriving on Delta Station, I was unable to finish my meal.

GATHERING

The synthetic silk we simply knew as synthsilk was probably the most expensive thing I owned. It had been a gift from an early admirer who had more money than he'd had brains. It probably didn't hurt that his female companion was fond of watching us make out. Must have made it worth her wallet.

The fabric moved over my skin like water, clinging to my chest and arms in a way that would tease, but another movement would make it a mystery once more. The dark blue fabric contrasted with my skin. I ran a hand over my hair, wishing it wasn't regulation short. There was just something wonderful about the look of a man's hair when he'd just been fucked. I wanted to look like that. Oh, well. My current appearance would have to serve. I slid on a pair of black trousers that left no questions about how fine my ass was and sauntered out the door with my invitation in hand.

My heart pounded as I arrived in the exclusive levels of the Station. I was allowed in only when I presented my invitation. The officer at the front was a young man with dark locks and full lips. His green eyes reminded me of Eric. I hated the fact such things made me think of him now when I was trying to forget him.

The officer took out a slender metal device, what appeared to be pointer, and directed a blue light on the silk card I held in my hand. The blue revealed the previously invisible acceptance. The officer gave me a tiny smile and nudged his head for me to go right in.

"Enjoy," he whispered.

The escorts were young, mostly lower-ranking officers, who were trying to get their feet in the door. It was an honor to be allowed to be among the older and wiser commanding officers, who only wanted a pretty face to mentor or merely have by their side. One night would do for some, but for others the invitation was for a lengthy relationship. Eric and I had met at a party such as this. Our relationship had blossomed and had lasted for two years. These parties were the sort of events to get one among the officers, that could lead to a rise up the ranking ladder.

Only the best escorts attended. People as important as Admiral Patrick were invited to mingle among superiors and entertain them. Their interest in us would serve as a chance to advance into a better position among the Imperial Armed Forces. Whether we were good at charming or just looked enticing, it could work for us, we could earn a place.

I joined a group of others, eyeing my competition for the evening. My confidence swelled in my chest. There were a few I would have been happy to train with, but I knew I had something they didn't. I wanted Admiral Patrick with every fiber of my being. I'd changed my life to chase him. They were just here for a job. I knew I would fight for the place by his side if I had to.

The party was already in full swing when I entered the room. The room was lit with lamps shining in a variety of colors: burgundy, blue, hints of purple. Colors that cast lights across people's skin and made them look mysterious.

Perhaps I should have worn a lighter color, I thought pulling at the hem of synthsilk shirt. As I moved in closer, I realized my concern wasn't entirely necessary. Other than the lamps and the carpets, the furnishings were cream. If we were pressed up against them, we could be shown off to our best abilities.

A band of alien musicians played in the corner. Android servants served drinks and rolled around the room delivering finger foods and appetizers. This was some soiree; they'd even gone for a real singer—an alien female with a beautiful voice. I had seen her perform on a moon at the nearby Station in Victoria. I was surprised to see her here; she must have been gaining popularity with quite a large group of cadets who frequented the taverns. She was beautiful with a pastel blue skin. Scaly black dots covered the side of her face like freckles. Her hair was swirling curls of blue. She wore a red, sparkling dress that looked lovely on her.

My mind tried to wrap around the theme. It seemed to simply be refinement. She made me feel at ease. Simply hearing her sing calmed me. I no longer felt like a piece of meat being eyeballed by older commanding officers who only wanted a one-night-stand.

The top brass, human and otherwise, lounged around the room, glasses in their hands filled with liquids in a variety of colors. As my cohort of escorts spread out, they were quickly scooped up by older men, approached quickly like delicious desserts on a table. Others, such as myself, had their eyes on certain commanding officers and moved in immediately to beat any opponent to their target. At a far side of the room, I caught sight of two escorts racing to the same commanding officer, they were vicious vipers with one another. It was a furious competition, at least from as far as I could see. The commanding officer had their choices too, and they were just as furious in getting what they wanted.

I sought out my target. There he was. At the bar,

sipping a glass of something amber. He had dressed down for the evening in casual clothing. It made sense why I hadn't spotted him right away. This is what he looked like out of uniform. He was more dressed then down, though. He still had the metal displaying the uniform of the Imperial officer. But it was less restrictive, I supposed.

I could already feel desire pooling in my stomach. Admiral Patrick was finally going to see me tonight. I was going to be in his bed. I didn't even bother to bat my eyes at any of the others in the room as I made my way over to him. Something in the way I moved must have caught his attention from the corner of his eye. He looked at me; I could see his eyes grow a little wide. The telltale dart of a tongue on a lower lip.

"Hello," I said as I approached him.

A smile spread across his face as his gaze raked over me as subtly as if he'd touched me. There was another gaze pinned on me, however, and I could feel it boring into my back.

"Armstrong, you didn't tell me you had such a creature in your arsenal," said Admiral Patrick. My heart rate skyrocketed. I shifted slightly and stepped closer to the Admiral's body.

Commander Armstrong was looking at me like a man who was about to bash me over the head and drag me off to his cave. The desire was blatant in his stare. I tried to keep my face still. It would be to my advantage if he thought I still liked him, but then again, did it matter now that I had the Admiral right in front of me? His eyes told me that it didn't.

"Commander Armstrong and I are just friendly, Sir. I'm actually here alone." I said immediately, surprising both Armstrong and myself.

Did I dare? His eyes said everything his words wouldn't. He was both disappointed and angry.

He'd been absent from my life since Admiral Patrick had arrived. After all, it was his arrival that had preceded the Emperor's entrance with his consort. An Imperial cadet had been assigned to her for the time she was here. A young guy, new but quite skilled. From what I had understood through Station gossip, he was being very attentive.

I glanced around. Armstrong was looking for Captain Periz. Ah, there she was, pink skinned and standing beside another of her species. I wondered what they talked about. They were creatures that appeared to have no personality or free will. Did they talk at all or did they find it illogical? I didn't miss the way her eyes fell on me and Armstrong.

I gave her a haughty lift of my brow and turned back to the Admiral. He was the one I wanted. I could easily ignore Armstrong's meaty hand on my ass when Admiral Patrick's beautiful eyes were taking me in. "I don't believe we've been introduced. Where do you come from?" he asked. I was twining around his finger, twisting a little lip over at him to cast the desires I felt for him.

"Nowhere particularly interesting." I gave a practiced lift of my shoulder. Footsteps sounded on the floor behind us. Captain Periz was coming up behind to talk to Armstrong. I heard their voices even though they were whispering.

I didn't hear what was said, though. I threw a glance over my shoulder and could feel Armstrong looking at me again. Armstrong grumbled and left with her, leaving me with my Admiral at last.

"So, what is your name?" Admiral Patrick asked as I turned to give him my attention. Aware I was suddenly alone with him my hands began to shake. The gap of my mouth dropped slightly as I forced my lips to move and answer his question.

"Gab," I said before I corrected myself quickly, "Gabriel." His lips curved into a lovely smile.

"That's a beautiful name," he said.

Typically, I found this line to be overused, generic, and annoying, but when he used it, I was able to overlook all that.

"Lovely, would you like to join me?" he asked. He grinned and put his drink down on the bar. All around, the crowd of officers and cadets had settled in with their choice of suitors. Those that were still looking glanced in my direction, hoping I would bat my eyes back at them. I threw away their glances and returned my eyes to the Admiral. I answered, "I would like that."

The Admiral extended his forearm out. I took his

lead. I was surprised he was guiding me out of the party, away from the gathering that he was hosting. I had thought that he had wanted me to sit with him and converse, but we were walking into the corridor. I said nothing, but smiled victoriously.

IN HIS QUARTERS

It was surprisingly easy to get him into bed with me. Maybe it was that I had over-prepared or maybe it was just that he was just drawn to the curve of my ass and the way my body drew against the synthsilk. It was what the parties were for, after all— to get the important people pliant and sated for negotiations. I was on offer, and oh was I willing to give. It was a subtle gesture, but with just enough hesitation that I knew he didn't do this often. I gripped his fingers back, pleased that I was the one that had made it to his notice.

We left the party with its noise behind. I caught a glimpse of Armstrong and Captain Periz standing near the mistress. Armstrong looked downright distraught. *Whatever*, I thought. I wasn't concerned about him, not now when I was about to have the person I had done all of this to achieve. As soon as the door closed between us and the party, the silence made it so every little motion could be heard. The movement of his slick dress shoes on the carpet. My short breaths of anticipation. The soft thumps and sounds from the rooms with closed doors. He didn't stop at the first open door, but walked all the way to the end. He pulled a keycard from his pocket and slipped it in. Apparently, the Admiral had his own special room. He gestured for me to step in first: a soft, guiding hand at the small of my back. The door whooshed shut behind him and I swore I could hear my own heartbeat. I looked at him, ready for him to lay hands on me, but he only smiled and walked further into the room.

"Make yourself comfortable," he said.

I was taken aback. This wasn't protocol in the slightest. Confused, I settled down on the couch, legs spread, an easy invitation. He watched me for a moment and then went to the panel on the wall and typed in an order. A moment later, the cabinet whirred open, and two glasses and a bottle of amber liquid was there. "Oh, I should have asked. Do you prefer whiskey, or would you like something else?"

"Anything that pleases you."

I hoped I was imagining the little crease that appeared between his brows. He walked over and sat in the reclining chair. There was a table between us where he set the glasses and poured a finger of liquor into each. "So, why are you here? I expect an actual answer, not a Companion's written response."

All right, now I was confused. "My name is Gabriel Heinrich."

"And where did you come from?" he repeated his earlier question before I could continue.

"A little Station of no importance."

"What was your profession before you came here?"

What was this, a job interview? "I really did not have one. I could never turn my hand to any one thing, except pleasure, which is why I became a recruit." I picked up my glass, tilting it this way and that. After Captain Periz had pulled her trick and after Armstrong had had his way with me, I was always worried about some mysterious powder clinging to the glass. None visible, I threw it back.

"Did you have a lover?" He threw back his own drink. I hesitated. "The truth, Gabriel."

"Yes, but I left him."

"Why?"

"I had a lot of reasons, some that make more sense as days go by and others that don't."

He leaned back in his seat, his own legs spread wide. I wanted to crawl between them. I let my desire for him show on my face. "To be honest, Sir, one of the reasons I left was...you." The words had tumbled out of my mouth and I immediately wanted to take them back. He probably didn't want a sycophant. His brow furrowed.

"I think I remember you," he said.

Remembered me? I couldn't recall how or when we had come face to face for him to remember me. Had I missed him admiring me from a distance?

He poured another drink in his hand. "Come here, Gabriel." I liked the way my name sounded on his lips and I think he liked saying it. He would turn over my name like he was sucking on a sweet fruit. Man, I wanted him to suck on something else.

I came over, standing in front of him. He reached out and caught me by my synthsilk shirt, tugging me forward. I came and settled into his lap. He put a hand on my hip as I straddled him and tipped up his glass with another hand. I could see the flush of the alcohol spread on his cheeks. I took the glass from his fingers and leaned forward, tasting the lingering liquid on his lips. It burned through me. The glass clattered onto the table next to the chair, but the sound barely registered in my mind.

His hands were big, warming the fabric of my shirt as he slid one up my back to grip the back of my head. For the second time, I wished I had longer hair again. To feel the tug of his fingers on my scalp would have heated me in all the right places.

I felt that giddy feeling that I'd had the first time I'd ever touched another person like this. I couldn't even remember his name now and there had been so many others. It was the feeling of anticipation, and then having the object of desire stick their tongue down your throat and slide their hands beneath your clothes. When the kiss began, he was unsure, but by the end of it he was grasping me with a possessiveness I didn't know existed. The possessive I had missed in Eric when he used to do that to me before he was tamed. *Why was I thinking of him now?*

He tipped me backwards, so I had no recourse but to wrap my arms around his back to keep from tumbling off the chair. My legs wrapped around him, grinding us together. His lips pulled away from mine, so that he could lay claim to my throat, pulling aside the collar of my shirt to taste my skin. I ground my groin against his stomach so he could feel how hard I had become. He moaned against the damp skin of my throat. He shifted, getting a better grip on me as he stood up from the chair. From his wiry frame I had never guessed at his strength. He set me unsteadily on my feet.

"Take your clothes off," he ordered, breath hot against my ear. It was one order I was happy to comply with. I stepped back from him and paused for only a moment to decide where to start. I pushed off my shoes and kicked them beneath the chairs. Then, came my dress socks. Trousers next. I was slow with this part, sliding the dark fabric over my legs.

I glanced up at him from beneath my eyelashes.

"Perhaps you could help me, Sir?" He actually

blushed. I felt it in every fiber of my being. He knelt down, his dress clothes wrinkling against the plush carpet. He put his hands on my bare thighs and took the fabric out of my hands, drawing it over my calves and ankles. His touch was light. When it ghosted back up my legs, I thought I was going to lose my ability to stand. He pressed his thumbs into the soft skin where my legs met my hips. He pushed up my shirt and, for a moment, I thought he was going to touch my straining cock. Instead, he pressed a warm, open mouth kiss to my stomach. My knees trembled. He stood up, fingers leaving my skin.

"Now, the shirt."

I tried to keep the trembling in my limbs under control as I lifted the hem. The smooth fabric lifted off me, leaving me bare to his gaze. I let the fabric drop from my fingers and lie where it pooled on the floor. That spark that I had seen at the bar was back in his eyes. It was there for an instant before being replaced by the cool picture of control. He stepped away from me, putting the chair between us. "Get on the bed."

I did as I was told, trying to arrange myself in an invitation that he would need to take. Everything about him fascinated and confused me even further. He wanted me; I could tell. However, he wasn't in a hurry. Armstrong, that overbearing jerk, was always in a hurry. He brushed his fingers on the neck of the glass bottle as though considering another drink, but he stepped away from it before indulging in the alcohol.

"Watch me," he said. I didn't really need to be asked. His fingers were swift and efficient on his own clothing. He wanted me to see him and take him in. Chest first, broad and compactly muscled, a large scar over the right side of his abdomen. There was a pucker from a blast wound on his left shoulder. That was probably the shot he'd taken for the Emperor years ago. The hairs on his chest were wiry and my fingers twitched with the desire to run through them. His military belt dropped from his fingers to clatter on top of my shirt. I moved, wanting to take the hem of his trousers into my own hands, drag them down his legs, grasp at his underwear and free him. He shook his head when he saw me move. With more theatrics than I would have given the stern man credit for, he pulled down his trousers and paused at the hem of his tight boxer briefs. I could see the jut of his dick. I licked my lips.

He didn't remove them, but got up onto the bed between my spread knees and bent me over backwards with a kiss. Again, his fingers fought for purchase in my short hair as I wrapped my legs around him and ran my fingers up his sides. I fought for patience in myself as my skin rubbed against his underwear. The hairs on his legs tickled the inside of my thigh. "Fuck me," I said in his ear.

He groaned against my shoulder.

I reached between us, palming him through the fabric. I wasn't the only one trembling. I slowly grasped the hem of the fabric and began pushing it down over his hips. He didn't stop me. His skin was velvety soft in my hand as I stroked him. His mouth was warm and wet on my throat, on the lobe of my ear.

"Make love to me, Gabriel."

I paused. I didn't think it was possible for me to blush anymore, not after some of the things that I'd done. No one had said something like that to me since Eric. My fingers found his jaw and tilted his face toward mine. That vulnerable look was in his eyes again. Was this what love felt like? Yes, I saw the same look in Eric's eyes. I wasn't sure about love anymore, but I wanted a taste of it again.

My lips found his and I pushed him back onto the blankets, pulling the last bit of cloth out of the way. The Admiral was older than me by at least a decade. I could see the lines in his face and a few gray hairs at his temples. His fingers scrambled at the shelf above the bed, finding one of the bottles of lube which he handed to me. The gel was cold on my fingers, but soon warmed up between our bodies as I probed. It had been a long time since I'd been on top. Suddenly, I wanted to take it slow. I crooked my finger inside him and watched him squirm.

I began to work my way down his body, his knees hooking over my shoulders I took him in my mouth.

This was something I was more familiar with, the heavy weight of a cock in my mouth. My body knew this; I could detach my brain to think of how best to please him further. The sounds my Admiral made ratcheted up my own desire and soon I was sliding back up his body, my own cock slicked with the warm gel so that I could nudge it between his legs.

"Face to face?" I asked, wondering if he would be comfortable bent that way. I didn't want to hurt him. He nodded, drawing my tongue into his mouth and pulling my hips closer. It took what little shred of control I had left not to come on the first thrust. He was warm and tight, and it had been so long! He wanted it slow and deep. I gave it to him for as long as I could hold out.

He came. I tumbled over the edge after him, dropping from the shivering force in my arms. I fell against his chest. He ran his fingers over my skull, touching me as if I was something special, fragile.

We'd cleaned up and crawled back into the bed, my head on his chest.

"You remind me of someone special, Gabriel," the Admiral said while we were lying together in bed. He squeezed me tightly against his body. He had loved before. Someone as gentle and loving had to have loved fiercely, I knew that.

I gazed up at him. His deep brown eyes met mine. The lines on his face made him wiser. Though older, he was incredibly attractive.

"I had a lover once, too. You actually remind me of him a little... When I first saw you, I thought..." He became silent, perhaps he had said too much. He looked broken suddenly. Had he hurt him or lost him? "I saw the same innocence in your eyes. It made me think of him."

That explained a lot. I tried not to think too much about how he'd only chosen me because of a reminder of a broken heart from someone he missed.

"What happened to him?" I was curious. Who was this person that distracted him and took him away from me? It made me a bit jealous to have him long for him when he was here with me.

He hesitated. I thought that he would not talk about it, that he didn't want to. "It's complicated... It made things hard between us..." He thought for a moment. He appeared to be holding back. I felt bad that I had asked. However, that didn't make me less curious.

"I'm sorry I shouldn't have pried."

He smiled and caressed my forehead. "No don't be. If anyone should apologize, it should be me to you. Why would you want to hear about some lost lover of mine, right?" He grinned, trying to laugh it off.

"No, I don't mind. I'd very much like to hear it. If you want to talk about it, that is."

He was quiet again, staring deeply into my eyes. "Very well." He pressed his lips inward. "I did something that separated us. I blame myself." His hand went to the large scar on his side. My fingers tangled with his as we traced it. "It was for the best, I guess..."

He was a liar; he was still mourning his lover. I could see it all over him.

"I'm sorry I asked." I made myself say the words. It felt like too raw a truth to be whispering after casual sex. His fingers brushed across my belly.

"Don't be. It's done. It's all in the past now."

I didn't believe it, which made me think of my relationship. *What if Eric was in another's arms saying the same things? Talking about me to another suitor?* That made me quiver slightly. I didn't want to admit it. It made me jealous to think of him in someone else's arms.

"What about you? What happened? What made you leave your..." he paused. I guess it was my turn to be asked why I was in the arms of another man.

I didn't know what to say. Quite frankly, there was regret in me now. What he had lost was nothing like what I had lost. I had lost it by my own doing, by being selfish. Sure, I didn't know his reasons, but they couldn't be as bad as mine. I said the first thing that I felt. "I didn't feel worthy."

"Do not be so quick to write yourself off as one who isn't good. We always have a chance to surprise ourselves."

My heart twisted. I couldn't believe I had said

those very words. Maybe he was right. Maybe it was love, or something like it.

We fell asleep wrapped up in each other's arms and arose late the next day. He took me in the shower, but then it was back to preparing to go back to our roles. He was an Admiral; I was a technical officer. Suddenly, I wasn't all that satisfied with my position. Most of all, my night with him seemed less than I expected. For so long I had dreamed of the moment we would have together. I had done it; I had spent a night with him, but it seemed small in comparison to what I had left behind. Now, I could truly see what I had lost.

"I hope we meet again, Gab," he said. Drawing near, he kissed me suddenly on the cheek. It was a kiss one gives a lover, not a one-night-stand. It made me wonder. The odd thing about the stare he gave me was there, but there was another person in his eyes. He wasn't looking at me. He was looking at someone else from his past. He was thinking of that lost love again.

"If you ever have need of anything, let me know." He pressed a data chip into my hand, and I slipped it into my pocket. "Next time I arrive on this Station, I will certainly call upon you." He drew me into one last kiss and then we walked down opposite hallways. I stopped to watch him disappear from my life and back into the role of Admiral.

Alone in that hall there was no one to flash a victory smile to, but I felt so victorious.

———

"DID you see that threat that was published in the news feeds?" said Aiden, announcing it to the table full of escorts as we picked at our salads at dinner. We glanced up and he caught my eye. There were a few beauties among us, none that I had made friends with, though. The only one I knew a little was Aiden and I was starting to question his friendliness towards me.

"Threat?" I asked, not in the least bit curious. I smirked a little recalling the night with the Admiral. I wanted to reveal that little secret to the others, but knew such a thing would likely not go well with them. They were all furious little jealous things.

"There has been a letter published saying that the prophecy will come true. Someone has targeted the visiting mistress to die." There were a few murmurings around the table. I barely looked up, more focused on concentrating on my meal.

"What does that have to do with us?" asked one of the girls whose name I couldn't remember. Blue Streak, that's what I called her in my head, well, until she'd changed it to green.

"We are privy to the intimate persons of high officials, what if there was an assassination attempt?"

"Well, you don't have to worry about that, Aiden." Green Streak laughed. "It's not likely the mistress is going to be calling on you."

"No, but she is going to be calling on Commander Armstrong," he said. Armstrong, from what I had heard, had been assigned to the mistress and her escort. He was a young guy, handsome and cocky.

"I would have trusted the Imperial officer before the commander to protect anyone, especially the mistress," another escort said over their laughter. I totally agreed with him.

"I doubt she would agree she would call on Armstrong for anything." I found her choice of him surprising, considering the man had a better aptitude for dicks. "For protection that is." I clarified, lowering my fork.

Aiden was giving me a look, trying to tell me something. I didn't know what on earth he could be saying. I'd been avoiding Armstrong's lustful gazes ever since Admiral Patrick left. That sweating hulk just didn't appeal to me after Patrick, no matter what position I could get from him.

I finished my salad and got up, giving Aiden the chance to get up and follow me. If he wanted to tell me what he was thinking, he could just damn well explain himself. I emptied my tray, set it in the cleaning belt, and moved out of the chew hall. I could hear his footsteps in the hall behind me. We walked into one of the empty offices. "What?"

"You're close to Admiral Patrick and we both know your position with Commander Armstrong."

"And?" I said pressing my lips together and crossing my arms.

"And we need you to get information."

"Who needs information?"

"Certain individuals."

"No way, I'm not into intrigue or political nonsense."

I turned to walk away, but Aiden grabbed me. I was just about to lay him flat when he said, "You want out?"

My nose wrinkled back at him. What the heck did that mean? He noticed the confusion on my face.

"The same person who wanted you drugged and pliable may be behind it," he revealed.

"Periz?" I growled, biting the side of my mouth and hurting myself.

"If you wanted revenge on her, now would be the time." Aiden examined the nails of one hand, his face nonchalant.

I froze. *Why was he helping me? And what did he want?* I stared at him, want curling in my gut. That woman humiliated me. She tricked me. Her pink alien face haunted the hallways of this Station. She tried to stand in the way of me and Admiral Patrick. I could see that she wasn't going to pull Armstrong away until the Emperor had prodded it, but what was her angle? She struck me as the kind of person that was looking out for herself. What was she getting out of helping someone like Armstrong? I didn't care, but I knew it had to be more. Against my better judgement, I asked, "What would I need to do?"

"Get Armstrong into bed at this time and date. He needs to be thoroughly distracted," Aiden said.

I cringed. Wasn't there any other way? "What?!" I glared back at him with a twist to my lip. "Couldn't you do it?"

He shot me a quick stare. We both knew who would fool Armstrong faster, who he wanted more. *Me,* of course. I knew it, so did Aiden, even Periz knew it.

"I had to take care of him while you were in bed with the Admiral. I did my duty, it's time to do yours."

"Excuse me?" I just about sprang at him from my place. Since when was it my duty to seduce that...I held in what I meant to say or do. "Fuck you!" I said.

I meant to walk away, but his voice stopped me. "I would hate for poor Commander Peterson to get the wrong idea about you."

I stopped suddenly and spun around to face him. I stared at him for a moment. His lips curled to one side cleverly. "What are you talking about?" Suddenly, I had a bad feeling and an idea what he meant.

"I might have taken a few images for myself of you and Armstrong. Captain Periz keeps the commander's quarters heavily monitored... for his protection of course."

"He would never believe it. If anything, it would prove he took advantage of me," I boldly said.

"Really?" He pulled out a chip and extended it to me. I snatched it from his hand immediately. "A little sample just for you. I think the images speak for themselves."

I realized he was right as I glanced at the image in the image reader. The images showed quite the opposite of what I had decided had happened with Armstrong. From the photo footage, I was not a victim, merely a cheater who had been caught in the act. I huffed in defeat. These assholes had me bent over a barrel.

I took the paper he had with the date and time on it. Tomorrow night.

"This will thwart Captain Periz how?"

"You'll see," Aiden said with a nod. I nodded back and we went our separate ways.

I was awash with confusion. I thought of the data chip that I had locked away in the private box in my room. Admiral Patrick's data. The information that could get me out of here and anywhere in the galaxy. I should have asked. I still could. But Captain Periz would still be out there working whatever game she was working.

No, she had to fall.

THE FALL

I turned a corner and froze midway as I caught sight of him, my heart skipped a beat, fear settled inside me. He was *here*. But why? Obviously, it wasn't for me. Eric was a commander; he had a professional career that involved more than just me. I saw him among other commanders and other officers. They were walking through the ship docking bay looking at the men working. His eyes wandered around a few times, *was he looking for me?* They must be here to oversee the construction of the new aircraft. It was a new fighter ship, and he and the other commanders had the honor of inspecting it before it would actually be presented to His Highness. He looked stunning. Strangely, he didn't see me. I honestly didn't want him to. I avoided his gaze by moving behind the metal body of a fighter ship. I was too ashamed to be seen, too embarrassed. I feared he would have me brought to him, but if he wanted to give me my space, he might not. That thought was comforting.

Eric looked so badly torn and hurt. Had I really had that effect on him? Had I really been the cause of his disheveled appearance? He appeared tired and lost. He was but a mirror image of his former self. That was my fault.

My night with Admiral Patrick had been playing over and over in my mind like an earworm. There was no getting around it this time. It had affected my professionalism. When once I thought I was in love with the Admiral, I wasn't sure any longer, after seeing Eric so destroyed.

I turned a corner once it was clear to continue. I knew where Armstrong was going to be. The escorts were pretty good at keeping tabs on the more interesting officers. All I had to do was ask the right questions.

They assumed I was smitten with him. It was a thought that made me sick to my stomach, but I was able to hide it. He was with some other officers in the rec lounge. No way he was going to stay there for long, though. He was never one to stay put.

As I walked, I tried to figure out how to get him away from the others. It couldn't be too obvious, of course; attracting attention would be bad. I turned a corner. I couldn't think of anything.

Come on, I told myself. *Think! This is important.*

Another corner. My heart was making strange movements in my chest. "Captain Periz needs to be taken down," I muttered. One more step. Another. Another. "I can do this."

I stopped, leaning against the wall. "I can't do this."

All I could think about was what Armstrong did to me. Whatever Aiden had planned, it was not worth it. Why didn't Aiden do it? He didn't even let me know what information they needed or how they were going to get it.

I turned, damn near running. With every step I took away from Armstrong, my heart become calmer and calmer. When I turned another corner, I bent over and breathed deeply as if I'd been running a marathon.

It was time to head to my quarters. With luck, the commander would keep himself busy and out of Aiden's hair. Aiden might not even notice I didn't do my part. Not that I cared what Aiden thought.

I straightened up and started back to my quarters. I kept my face a blank mask for all the people I passed. This was one of the longest journeys I'd ever taken, and it was just across one single ship.

When I got to my quarters, the mask shattered. I

tasted bile in my throat. I slid down to the floor with my back against the wall.

I'd had no idea that I was still so affected by what had happened. After a few deep breaths, I got to my feet and headed back outside. I didn't want to be alone right now.

I headed straight to the quarters I knew so well. I pressed the buzzer and waited. No answer. I pressed again. Still nothing.

Where was he? Part of me wondered if he was in the rec lounge with Armstrong. That thought made my stomach sink. With a sigh, I turned to leave.

Suddenly, for reasons I couldn't understand, I stopped walking. I turned the other way, heading towards the Admiral's quarters. *What am I doing?* I asked myself.

My pager suddenly beeped. I lifted the fingernail-sized device from my belt and the mechanical voice spoke. "Technical Officer Gabriel Heinrich, please report to the infirmary."

Infirmary?

Who would be in there? I had no next of kin on the ship. If anyone was sick or hurt, why would the med staff be calling me?

Still, I left the door to Admiral Patrick's room and headed straight there, all the while trying to figure out who could be waiting for me.

On my way, I almost ran into someone as I turned

a corner. "Aiden? What are you doing here?" I bel-
lowed. "Where are you going in such a hurry? What
the fuck is going on?" I demanded again.

Aiden stood there, staring at me with wide eyes.
"Doing my job," Aiden bit back. "Unlike you.
Weren't you supposed to be with Commander
Armstrong?"

I gritted my teeth. "What? Is your reconnaissance
mission not going as planned? Did Armstrong find
out what you were doing?"

"No," Aiden answered quickly. "Just get back to
it. We're not done yet."

Without another word he rushed past me and
vanished around a corner. I stared after him for a few
seconds, then I turned and continued towards the
infirmary.

———

WHEN I ENTERED THE INFIRMARY, Admiral
Patrick was there waiting for me, standing right in the
middle of the room. The beds to the right were covered by a single drape.

"Officer Heinrich," he said, walking up to me.
His voice sounded so professional it caught me off
guard. The doctor and nurse stood where they
were, deferring to him. Imperial soldiers stood on
guard.

"What's going on? Are you hurt?"

"No," Admiral Patrick answered. "I'm fine. It's..." He sighed and stood aside. I heard a groan.

My heart nearly stopped. "Eric," I whispered. *My Eric.* He lay on a bed, unconscious. There was an IV hanging on the wall leading to his arm. I rushed to his side and held his hand. He didn't move.

"He's going to be fine," the medic said.

"What happened?" I asked.

Admiral Patrick placed a hand on my shoulder. "He was drugged. Some sort of date rape drug. He apparently had an adverse reaction, though." He exhaled slowly, his hand curled around my shoulder in comfort. "Also, there was something else... We found Imperial files accessed through his technical devices. Someone hacked the files and was able to gain access to important information."

My mouth dropped into a gap and soon something came to realization. The commander wasn't the one Aiden wanted to distract. The gap of my mouth widened. *I was.* He knew Eric had access to important documentation. He knew I would never allow anything to happen to Eric.

Eric being a higher-ranking commander could easily have classified information pertinent to him that Armstrong didn't have. It would be easier to gain access to. I knew that much; it was one of the many reasons I had fallen for him. His rank, his power... There was more that attracted me to him now, but I didn't care what it was.

My heart started beating too fast. Seeing Eric like this brought back memories of when it happened to me. The helplessness, the shock...

This was all going too fast. The Admiral said more, but I didn't hear any of it. My mind was elsewhere.

"It was Aiden, wasn't it?" I said, interrupting him. "He did this." I should have known. All this secrecy; the supposed individuals who wanted information, a vague plan to bring Captain Periz down. I let hopes of revenge blind me. Had Aiden's plans ever included her?

He'd seemed strange when I saw him. His normally cool, calculated demeanor was gone. He'd told me to keep Armstrong busy, but Armstrong wasn't the one he wanted distracted. I was. Aiden had tricked me.

Admiral Patrick said nothing at first. Then, "I found Eric stumbling in the corridors. He did mention Aiden's name before he went unconscious, yes. I called security and told them to be on the lookout for him. All shuttles and escape pods are being monitored, as well. There's no escape for him."

Don't be so sure, I thought.

I got to my feet and headed out the door. The Admiral asked me where I was going, but I didn't answer. He said something to the med staff and then was right on my tail along with three Imperial soldiers.

"Do you have the schematics for the ship?" I asked.

"Of course, I do." The Admiral lifted a chip from his belt and a holographic map appeared above it. He handed it to me.

Good. It had more than just the location of every room and pathway on the ship; it included notes and schedules. I searched for where I'd run into Aiden. Based on the direction he had hurried off to, one possible destination was...

"He's headed for the cargo bay. There's a cargo shipment scheduled for tomorrow morning. If Aiden got onto one of those crates, then he'd be packed onto the shuttle and be home free."

"Isn't that a bit of a long shot?" The Admiral said.

"Yeah, but it's still a shot," I answered. "I am *not* going to let him get away."

"Gabriel," Admiral Patrick said, "I get it. You're angry. You have every right to be. But—"

"No!" I turned to him. "I don't need another psychotherapy session right now. What I need is Aiden caught. I need answers."

I handed the chip back to him and stormed off.

When I got to the cargo bay, I immediately felt the hope dissipate. The room was huge. There were so many crates that there was no way I'd be able to search them all. Even if I could, and Aiden was in there, chances were high he'd be able to sneak away while I was searching the boxes.

Admiral Patrick came up behind me and the Imperial officers scattered at his command. "You really think he's in here?"

I didn't answer.

"Okay. I picked up something on the way." He handed me a pair of goggles, keeping a pair for himself. Heat-sensitive goggles. He led the way.

I kept my eyes peeled for any heat signature. Nothing. Everything looked gray through the glasses. The closer and closer we got to the scheduled crates, the more forlorn and angry I got.

"Here they are," Admiral Patrick said. "We'd be able to see heat signatures if he was inside any of them." Sure enough, all the crates looked dull gray through the goggles.

Then, I saw some red from the corner of my eye. A human-shaped redness. "There!" I yelled.

The Admiral ordered the officers to approach with him. I followed behind.

Aiden knocked over some crates, but there was no way that would stop me. I ran like my life depended on it, and eventually caught up to him. I jumped and pinned him to the floor. The Imperial officers approached and came up behind us, pinning Aiden's arms behind him. Admiral Patrick stood aside as they lifted him from off the floor to his feet.

"Why?" I screamed. "Why did you do it?" He frowned but said nothing. I punched him in the face. "Answer me!"

He spat blood, turned to me, and sneered. "Why do you think? She's got friends here, too, you know. You don't even know the half of what you've gotten yourself involved in. You know very little. How else to weaken you, but to make you think your beloved Eric had slept with someone else?" He smirked.

"That's what you did?"

He laughed. "Not even close."

I straightened up, staring down my nose at him. If it wasn't for the Admiral, I probably would have struck Aiden right in the stomach. Or the balls.

"Take him to the holding cells until the commanding council deals with him," the Admiral said. The Imperial officers dragged him away as Admiral Patrick promised: "This will be your last day of freedom for a long time."

When Aiden and the officers were gone, I felt the Admiral's gentle touch upon my shoulder, his finger pressed tightly. Slowly turning, he leaned forward to kiss me, but I stopped him.

"I can't," I said, surprising myself slightly. He hadn't taken my words seriously until he saw the look in my eyes.

He smiled warmly. It was nothing of what I expected he'd do.

"I understand. You love him."

I wasn't surprised that he knew. I mean Eric was there on the bed a mess and... I just couldn't. Was it any different from what he felt for the unknown lover that had taken him from me our first time together?

The Admiral put a finger against my lips. His eyes were moist and almost glazed over. He pulled me towards him and hugged me. "Thank you," he said.

I breathed in his scent. I could tell he was fine. Still here. Still with me.

"For what?"

He pushed me back and looked at me. "Gabriel. Being with you, even for a short moment, had a way of changing my perspective. I hope for the better, in this case." I gave him a quizzical look, and he continued. "Being with you, I felt... alive. For the first time in so long. You opened my eyes to the possibilities of change." He looked past me toward the large windows of the ship. I felt those viewports reminded him of something or someone. I kept my eyes on him. Soon, he turned his eyes back, realizing his distance.

"I guess what I'm saying is: Don't lose him. You love him. Go to him. Tell him. Stop running away from your feelings. What are you afraid of?"

My heart leapt. I swallowed what I wanted to say. My head dropped slightly; I hadn't even realized I was drawn into my thoughts. There really wasn't much to say. He was right. He lifted my chin so tenderly it caught me off guard.

He laughed. It was a deep laugh that shook his firm body.

"Don't worry about it." I smiled and nodded.

He hugged me tightly again and kissed me on the forehead, like I was a friend. It wasn't the chaotic tug of war I'd had with the commander. This was sensual, reaching deep into my heart and caressing it.

TOGETHER

I was packing my things and looking about at the room that I would leave soon for better accommodation when he entered. He seemed to be in good spirits. Quickly, I recalled why I had fallen so hard for him.

After the incident he had been given leave. It wasn't every day something so strange and horrible happened. Eric had been assessed by a counselor and found that he wasn't adversely affected by the event, but the therapist had recommended time for him to recover, nonetheless. I understood that. I wasn't sure I had ever gotten over being drugged.

Of course, Eric had pulled some strings to get me time off, too. I stopped packing and sat thoughtfully on my bed. All these things that had happened—being raped by a commanding officer, meeting and dealing with characters like Aiden and Periz. I wondered about her now, staring at my things. I feared she had something else up her sleeve. I never expected any of this to happen.

To think I had a second chance at love. A chance with someone who was not only a damn good fuck, but that I'd wanted in so many other ways. It had taken a long, confusing trip for me to realize it. The universe was actually smiling on me for once.

The investigation into Aiden and whoever was working with him was ongoing. I was prepared to give a testimony at his trial if they needed me to. It might not go so far, though; cameras had caught him and his partner heading to Eric's room. Part of me wondered what they wanted and if there were more people involved in their little plan. I wanted to interrogate Aiden myself, but, of course, it would be less of an interrogation and more of a beat-down.

Eric neared and I rose immediately before he had the chance to speak. I kissed him, then wrapped my arms around him. I held him to me for a long moment. I just wanted to feel him, let his scent and his warmth envelop me.

"I'm sorry," I whispered. I was trembling and I knew that he could feel it. I couldn't help it.

"Gab? What's wrong?" I pulled slowly away.

He stared into my eyes, tenderly stroking my face. I felt a pooling in my eyes.

"Gab, what is it?"

"I almost lost you. I'm so sorry I left. I'm so sorry I...if I hadn't been such a brat... none of this..."

He stopped me by putting a hand on my cheek. "Hey, stop that. Listen to me—" he wiped at my eyes tenderly. I leaned against his hand. "You did nothing. I don't blame you, and you shouldn't blame yourself. I wanted you to go and find yourself. I wanted you to be happy. I just hoped you'd come back." He smiled, caressing my cheek. "And look, you did. Your here with me now."

"Yes, Eric, I am." I wrapped my arms around him again. He held me for a long moment. Knowing deep inside I could have lost him, I kissed him and held him as if my life depended on it.

———

I FINISHED PACKING. I got to my feet and picked up my suitcase. Eric extended his hand as he stood to wait for me by the entrance of the room. Two Imperial officers stood a step away from him on the outer corridors of the ship. They were going to escort us to the landing bay.

"You're ready, darling?" Eric asked as I took his hand into mine.

I felt Eric grip my hand into his as he pulled me into the corridor, the men grabbed my things, and I took my place by Eric's side toward our awaiting ship.

"So where are we heading?" I asked curiously.

When I glanced over, his eyes met mine with a smile that stretched from ear to ear.

"Ever been to the tropical islands of Vertix?"

"Are those the tropical islands on that faraway planet where the sunsets last for hours?" I was giddy.

Eric laughed as he nodded. We were nearing the landing bay.

A large Imperial shuttle awaited us. The officers took our things onto the ship as we stopped at the entrance of the ramp. The pilot handed a flight schedule to Eric. Eric examined it, and after approving it, handed it back to the pilot who bowed his head and took the steps up the ramp.

"Well, are you ready, darling?" Eric asked. My heart lit up as I squeezed his hand. The co-pilot allowed us to enter first. I couldn't contain my excitement as we entered the shuttle craft.

Dear reader,

We hope you enjoyed reading *The Companions*. Please take a moment to leave a review, even if it's a short one. Your opinion is important to us.

Discover more books by C.S. Luis at https://www.nextchapter.pub/authors/cs-luis

Want to know when one of our books is free or discounted? Join the newsletter at http://eepurl.com/bqqB3H

Best regards,
C.S. Luis and the Next Chapter Team

The Companions
ISBN: 978-4-86747-888-2
Large Print

Published by
Next Chapter
1-60-20 Minami-Otsuka
170-0005 Toshima-Ku, Tokyo
+818035793528

28th May 2021

CPSIA information can be obtained
at www.ICGtesting.com
Printed in the USA
LVHW090440150621
690251LV00007B/199